The ten androids sat around the circular green table, still as metal castings.

Eight shone with a stainless steel finish.

Two—one male, one female—were a dazzling pale gold. These two metallic beings were so perfect that they seemed to have been cast by the hand of an alien-world Michelangelo. The golden male turned his eyeless oval head towards the Alphans. "You have been brought before the Council of Pelorus to give account of yourselves. You are deemed enemies."

Mastering his anger, Koenig replied, "I am Commander of Moonbase Alpha, and you know that we come in peace. Yet you viciously attack our base and savagely attempt to blow us out of space. It is *you* who must account for yourselves."

But the golden android turned his back on the Alphans. "You are doomed. We will destroy you."

ANDROID PLANET
was originally published by
Futura Publications Limited.

Books in the Space: 1999 Series

Published by POCKET BOOKS

ANDROID PLANET

JOHN RANKINE

PUBLISHED BY POCKET BOOKS NEW YORK

ANDROID PLANET

Futura Publications edition published 1976

POCKET BOOK edition published September, 1976

ISBN: 0-671-80706-4.

Printed in the U.S.A.

ANDROID
PLANET

CHAPTER ONE

The rhythm was long established. Simulated night followed artificial day in the sprawling complex of Moonbase Alpha. Memories of Earth planet were overlaid by all the living time that had been passed on the hurrying moon as she hurled herself deeper and farther into the vacant interstellar spaces.

After so long on their unlooked-for journey, personnel had come to terms with a way of life that hung on the thread of the life-support systems. The black velvet star map on the direct-vision ports and the halls and covered ways of Alpha were part of the furniture of every mind.

Commander John Koenig believed they would make out. Nothing in the action guaranteed it, or even supported it. But his sense of destiny was strong. Rightly or wrongly, he reckoned they could not have gotten this far to lose out to blind chance.

Waiting for chance to turn up the right card was harder at off-duty times. When they were on load, working at the endless chore of staying alive in a hostile environment, the personnel of Moonbase Alpha had enough to do to keep their minds at a stretch. Hydroponics staff in the food-producing sector, medics treating the sick in the well-found Medicentre, engineers, technicians, service staff: all could believe they were doing their thing in any unit anywhere on Earth planet. The fact that their hurrying platform was plunging through distances to make imagination sick was an academic point. Life had to be lived where it was drawing breath.

But when the watch changed and they went below, the plain truth was harder to ignore. There was no door to open. They were thrown back on their own resources. Computer could key them in to every kind of spectator pleasure, but it was no substitute for climbing the mountain or belting the ball for a full due down the fairway.

As much as possible, they opted for what they could do firsthand. The Time Out Committee ran leisure like an escaper's club. Some reckoned that the day would come when they would be found planning a tunnelling bid under the perimeter defence screens.

Commander John Koenig kept the power of veto. He knew the value of morale in an isolated enclave, but he knew, also, that when the chance came, as it surely would, there might be only minutes between the right decision and a miss. He wanted his people ready at all times.

When asked for his blessing on a theatrical venture, he gave himself a day to think about it and finally agreed with the proviso that they should pick something nonpolitical and that they should not ask him to be in it.

Choosing the production kept Moonbase Alpha in a turmoil for a week. Victor Bergman, Scientific Adviser to the base, who had gathered together a useful orchestra, wanted grand opera—something to tear at the living gut like *Bohème*. Alan Carter, Commander of the Eagle Fleet and earthy, was all for farce with Sandra Benes and Tanya, elegantly leggy co-workers in Main Mission, falling about in black lace pants. He said nobody, but nobody, could get away with "Your tiny hand is frozen" in the interstellar outback.

Dr. Helena Russell, Director of the Medicentre, was quietly pushing for a little class and some costume drama, seeing, in her mind's eye, this cool aristo in a sleek gown cutting down all and some with her barbed wit. So many men, so many opinions.

In the event, it was sorted out without anyone knowing where the decision had come from. Gilbert and Sullivan were at it again, in a setting neither would have believed possible. The brisk rhythms of *The Mikado* began to be tapped, hummed and whistled from the outlying sections to the beating heart of Main Mission. Koenig found fans dangling from wrists, and hand-printed fabrics being hastily shoved out of sight under operating consoles. Sandra Benes, a natural for Oriental make-up, appeared at her desk with her hair in a bird's nest and, clearly, only iron willpower kept her from speaking coyly from behind her fan.

The small recreation area could seat a hundred at a push. It was to be a three-night stand. When the opening night arrived, Koenig turned out in ceremonial rig with a fluted metal cloth tabard and sat in the front row.

Kano, who preferred playing chess with his computer, had elected to stand in with a scratch crew and keep Main Mission operational. He switched the endlessly searching probes to the monitor screens and had the interior of the recreation centre thrown up for all to see on the main scanner. They heard Bergman's theatre orchestra rip smartly through the overture and saw the curtain rise to the pomp and circumstance of the Japanese scene. Kano left his desk and walked slowly to the observation platform. Unfiltered by an atmosphere, the stars were bright and steady like so many jewels thrown on a black velvet pad.

Beyond the curve of the moon's bleak horizon, there was a faint pallor that brightened and dimmed as the moon yawed on her axis. He moved smartly to his own desk and took a bearing. He wrote it out and shoved it over to the girl at Sandra Benes's desk.

"Leanne, see what you can find at two-nine-one."

"Two-nine-one, check, Controller."

The long-range probes swung from their random

search and swept along the designated vector. There was a blip and a tiny, brilliant speck on the monitor screen.

Kano said, "Main scanner."

The opening chorus dissolved and the cheerful beat of the music cut dead. Main Mission was silent. Heads turned to look enquiringly at Kano. They had seen stars enough to last them for a long lifetime and they believed it was all done to show that the temporary controller was cracking the whip.

Kano's face was impassive. He waited for Leanne to go by the book and bring up the signal. By this time, Sandra Benes would have gotten it sorted. But, although Leanne was slow, she was steady. She made the final move and threw a switch. It was all there. A crewman said, "Holy Cow!"

Kano looked at it soberly. Set precisely in the centre of the big screen like a free-wheeling apricot was a small, yellow-orange planet, half screened by white cloud banks and circled by a glowing ring of pale viridian.

Kano had a problem. He would be nobody's friend if he sabotaged the show of the year for something that could wait a couple of hours with no loss. On the other hand, timing could be critical if the planet turned out to be the one they had been looking for.

He left Paul Morrow's command desk and slipped into his own vacant slot on the computer console. Data was already coming in. The outfall clattered and he tore off a tape.

SPHEROIDAL BODY: EQUATORIAL RA-
DIUS 4530.9 KILOMETRES: POLAR RA-
DIUS 4500: MEAN DISTANCE FROM SUN
150 MILLION: REVOLUTION ON AXIS 21
HOURS EARTH TIME: DUAL PLANETARY
SYSTEM . . .

He let the digestive process rumble on and punched another stud. There was a question he wanted to ask. Rapidly, he keyed in, "Do we have any record of this system on the *Voyager* tapes?"

A human operator would have said, "All right. Give me a break. I can't do it all at once."

Moonbase Alpha's master computer patiently disengaged a search circuit and began to whip through the archives. Material from the probing eyes of Earth's automated search ship *Voyager One* had been incorporated in the memory banks. It was an off chance that she had passed this way in the interstellar wilderness.

All of thirty-five seconds passed. In the computer room, the long panels flickered and glowed in a spasm of concentrated mental turmoil. Kano tapped the bland cowling close at hand and waited, conscious that all eyes in Main Mission had left the big screen and were on him. Somebody had to make a decision.

There was a discreet rumble from the hardware as the tin man cleared his throat. Kano flipped a switch to have a simultaneous broadcast and printout.

POSITIVE IDENTIFICATION. *VOYAGER* LOG: 6391143. SOLAR SYSTEM: OLYMPUS. PLANETS: PELORUS AND COPREON. . . .

There was a pause as a little matching went on and then:

THE PLANET ON 291 IS PELORUS.

The newcomer on the star map was gaudy as a lantern and Kano reckoned it would hang very well on the cyclorama. He used the comlock net for a one-to-one call to Koenig.

The buzz reached Koenig's ear under the umbrella of the Gentlemen of Japan rattling away at their opening chorus. He whipped out his comlock. On the miniature screen, Kano's face was impassive as an ebony mask. Keeping his voice low and feeling like a conspirator in a "B" movie, he said "Koenig."

"Commander. We have a solar system. Computer identifies. *Voyager* data on bank."

"Check. I'll be there. Get a printout for all sections."

Neighbours on the row were looking their question. Even some of the actors had seen the move and were missing the beat. Koenig made it slow as a reassurance that Alpha was in no danger of structural collapse and walked for the exit. Outside, he ran for a travel-tube exit to cut corners and save a long trek through the sprawling base.

The passenger tube clunked home and he was away, speeding for an entry point close to Main Mission. There was time to think that it was all beginning again. This was the way it would start. The long-range probes would pull in a picture. Sometime it would be the right one. Who could say that this might not be it?

He shoved all that to the back of his mind. There was a lot of mileage to make with routine investigation before they got around to a decision on whether or not they left the raft and committed themselves for all time. But it was there as a factor to make him impatient with the short delay. His own face stared at him from the polished hatch panel as he waited for the docking sequence. It was a dark, saturnine job: black hair, level brows, lines deepening round the mouth. In some ways it was the face of a stranger, but there was no time to chase that twist of thought to its hole. The hatch sliced away and he was out at a run.

Kano had gotten Pelorus nicely centred on the big screen, ripe as an autumn fruit. He said, "There she is, Commander."

Koenig came to a halt, feet astride, looking up at the screen. If the planet surface bore out the promise of its glowing colours, it would be something to see. First things first, he said, "What time do we have?"

"Six days, Commander. Extreme Eagle range in twelve hours. We pass close."

"How close?"

"Rough estimate only. Within the gravisphere. This will cause disturbance here and on the planet."

It was clear to Koenig that he needed the full Main-Mission staff on standby. He said shortly "General Alert. Command conference in fifteen minutes."

"General Alert. Check."

Strident klaxons sounded out in every outlying sector of Moonbase Alpha. Red telltales blinked on in every communications post. The base reacted like a disturbed hive. Victor Bergman stood on his podium with his baton raised, like a clockwork figure with a stuck spring. The auditorium emptied in an orderly stampede. A prudent stagehand brought up the house-lights and killed the floods. The bubble of illusion collapsed.

Main Mission slipped easily into top gear. Back at his post, Paul Morrow in mandarin rig moved his team through the drills of check and counter check. Data sheets piled up on the clipboards. When Koenig gathered the top brass in the command office, there was enough information swilling about to keep a research unit happy for a decade.

He looked round the circle of faces in some surprise. Except for Bergman, whose balding head and intelligent face was unchanged, they were all out of character. Helena Russell with kohl-rimmed eyes and a black wig looked all set to lure some Foreign Secretary to a diplomatic indiscretion. Making an effort, he stopped looking at her and started with a known and unchanged advisor. "Victor. You've had no time at all; but do you have any opinion?"

"We're lucky, John. The *Voyager* tape cuts some corners. Pelorus has a lot in common with Earth planet. It's at a similar developmental stage. There's a central core of iron and nickel, then a mantle of silicates supporting a thin crust. Atmosphere is twenty-two per cent oxygen. There's some argon, some carbon dioxide, a whole lot of inert gas which I haven't identified. If we can breathe it, there's no problem."

Helena Russell said, "I'm working on that. I believe it's all right."

Bergman went on, "The ring is an ionized layer. There could be trouble there, communicationswise, if we get an Eagle onto the surface."

There was the big question and nobody was getting to it. Koenig asked, "Life signs?"

Paul Morrow said, "Nothing on the monitors yet, Commander. But that isn't conclusive. We're a long way off."

Thinking aloud, Koenig said, "We'll get closer and that could sort itself out, but every hour that passes gives us less time for an in-depth investigation. Optimum time for transfer from Alpha would be in seventy-two hours. At that point conditions could be rough. How about that? Victor?"

Bergman flipped over a couple of data sheets and checked Computer's prediction. He was not looking happy. "Either way, John, it's going to be a stormy passage. This moon is travelling too fast to be pulled into an orbital path round Pelorus. But we'll change course, there's no doubt about that. If there are seas down there, they'll have freak storms that could wash out seaboard cities, if they exist. We won't be welcome, that's for truth."

"What about the effect on Alpha?"

"Hard to judge. We've weathered some shrewd knocks. There's no atmosphere to whip up a gale. There could be a shift of moondust."

Koenig left his command desk and walked to a direct-vision port. To the naked eye, Pelorus was now a brilliant dot lifted clear of the stark moonscape. When it came down to it, there was no substitute for a man getting off his ass and going to take a look. He walked slowly back. When he reached the desk, he had the decision clear. He said, "All right. This is what we do. Prepare for Operation Exodus. Evacuation of Moonbase Alpha timed seventy-two hours from now. Meantime I want a reconnaissance Eagle ready to lift off as soon as we have range. That's for you, Alan."

Alan Carter, Commander of the Eagle Fleet, cracked his oriental make-up in a broad grin. He said, "Check, Commander," and was half out of his seat as Koenig went on: "Assessment team of six: Victor for technical feasibility; Helena, medical; yourself, Alan; Paul for survey and logistics . . ." He saw the appeal in Sandra Benes's wide eyes and added, "Sandra on communications . . ."

Carter was clearly counting and had gotten five. He looked his question. Koenig said, "The sixth? I can't let you have all the pleasure. I'll be along to see you go the right way."

The conference broke up. Helena Russell, lithe and supple even in a voluminous kimono, came quickly to Koenig's side and touched his arm. Her eyes were startling under the strange black wig, as she said, "What do you think, John?"

"So far this planet is the best thing that's come our way. I'm keeping an open mind."

"They'll have seen us by this time."

"They?"

"The people. If there are people living there. Imagine if we were back on Earth and a moon appeared. How would we react?"

"By this time, we'd have worked out the likely effects. Cities drowned out. Devastation. We'd be opening deep shelters."

"How keen would we be to give sanctuary to travellers from the wrecker?"

"We'd understand they had no part in it."

"Some would, some wouldn't. It would depend on the culture level."

"The sooner we make contact the better."

A blip from the communications post made a period. Sandra's face appeared on the screen.

"Commander?"

Koenig shoved down a stud.

"Koenig."

"I have contact, Commander."

Koenig raced down the steps to the operations floor of Main Mission. Pelorus was filling the big screen from edge to edge. Sandra Benes threw a switch and what she had conjured out of the wasteland was loud and clear. Main Mission throbbed to a fantastic electronic beat. It had time and it had rhythm. It was organised noise.

Victor Bergman, the specialist, said "Music! We're dealing with an advanced culture."

Privately, Koenig reckoned that some very primitive communities had gotten around to beating a drum, but before he could speak, he saw Sandra Benes close her spectacular eyes and slip sideways to a point of no return.

Paul Morrow saw the movement and was calling sharply, "Sandra?" as he hurled himself across to catch her. He never made it. Mind blanked by the hammering rhythm, he reeled like a drunk and dropped to his knees. Kano slumped over the computer console. Tanya fell as she struggled to get to her feet. Koenig was a half stride from Sandra's desk when black night filled his eyes.

Main Mission was filled with the insistent beat, but the top brass of Moonbase Alpha were wrapped in a cloud of unknowing. The Eagle command console blipped urgently and Alan Carter's face appeared on the monitor.

"Commander?"

He might have been calling in an echoing vault.

"Commander? Do you read me? Eagle Six calling Main Mission."

He went through the sequence again, thumping his console with a gauntleted fist in the best tradition of a highly technical service. There was no joy. Using a direct link, he called the duty team in the bunker below the launch-pad silo. "Jake?"

"Captain?"

"What's with Main Mission? They don't answer."

Carter watched him try. He had a miniature picture of the inside of the bunker on the Eagle's scanner. Jake Henshaw, a slow moving but meticulous operator, stood at the communications post and tuned for a view into Main Mission. The picture within a picture was so small that Carter was leaning forward peering into it. Small and sharp edged, it was a scene from an oriental tomb. Flat on the deck, Paul Morrow had one arm outstretched and the tips of his fingers were centimetres away from Sandra's dark head. Kano, arms flung forward, was half lying on the presentation spread of his computer. Koenig had fallen and slid over the parquet, beating Paul to his target and touching the hem of Sandra's kimono.

Before he could check on the others, another factor entered the composition. For him, the signal was weak, but Jake was getting it strength nine. There was a rhythmic beat and a curious singsong note that seemed to be boring a hole in his head. Jake was hanging on to the fabric of the communications post and slowly slipping down to his knees.

Carter forced his hands to move and hit the key to cut the link. Then he was drawing long breaths and sitting tall in his pilot seat to clear the last trace of nausea from his gut.

Hunting round the channels, ready to switch out at a split-second's notice, he picked up the pilot's duty room and got Harry Negus who was on standby and was filling the unforgiving minute improving his manual skills on a miniature bar-billiards table. The urgent bleep spoiled his shot and his cue ball whipped down the no-score exit. With his expressive black face creased in a scowl, he stretched out a long arm for the communications post and put himself on the link.

It was an unnerving face to meet on a scanner, but Carter reckoned it was a whole lot better than what he had been getting.

"Harry?"

"The same. What is it, Chief?"

"Are you all right?"

Negus took a look at himself on the monitor. "Surely. All systems go."

"There's trouble in Main Mission. Don't switch on to their link. I'll be right with you."

The screen blanked. Negus used his comlock to open the hatch. The corridor outside was deserted. He shrugged and turned back to his table. It was all a mystery. He set the balls up again and was weighing the angles for a brilliant stroke when Carter was in with a rush.

"Get into a spacesuit and close the external mike."

It was not until he was ready to flip down his visor that Negus saw the problem.

"Chief?"

"What is it?"

"When I close up I won't hear a thing."

"That's right, so listen now. As I understand it, there's a signal going round Main Mission that's knocked all the personnel for six. Sealed up we might get inside and switch it off. When we get there, I'll go in and try it. I want you standing by outside. If you see me go under, you're to get the hell out of it and make for the power section. Kill power to Main Mission. If that doesn't work, you're on your own. All right?"

"I think so."

"Let's go, then."

Carter dropped his visor. Without the external pick-up he was in the world of the stone deaf. They went at a run for the nearest travel-tube exit and hurled themselves into a cage as the hatch opened.

Out again and getting close to the heartland of the sprawling complex, there was more evidence on the ground that the cancer in Main Mission was spreading out. A group of Alphans at an intersection round the communications post had folded where they stood. There was a leggy girl from Hydroponics balanced like an advanced yogi on her forehead and the balls of her feet.

Negus raised a bulky thumb as a tribute as he raced

by and then they were outside the Main-Mission hatch and Carter was warning him back.

Alan Carter used his comlock and the hatch sliced away. Mouth drying and a feeling of nausea building in his gut, he drove himself on. An etiolated whisper of the signal was getting through his acoustic barrier and he knew he could not take it for long. He made a beeline for Sandra's console and whipped along the keyboard, shoving every stud to Non Op.

The picture of the apricot planet dissolved in silver rain and the screen blanked and then filled again with the blue and white waiting sign of Moonbase Alpha. Sick and shaking, he leaned with both hands flat on the presentation table. He set himself to count slowly and reached twenty before he could tell for a truth that the effect was passing off. Cautiously he raised his visor. Except for the click and whirr of Kano's computer there was no sound in Main Mission.

Strangely, it had not occurred to him that they could all be dead. But suddenly the impact of the still figures made the point. Fumbling for the seals he tore off his gauntlets and knelt beside Sandra Benes. He zipped away the gay kimono, moving from ancient Japan to a very sophisticated, fishnet body stocking which was as good as covering the vital area with a grid reference. There was no need to plug her in to a life-sign monitor. The elegant Benes chest was expanding and contracting in a steady rhythm. She was still batting on the right side of the line that separates the quick from the dead.

Carter moved slowly back to the hatch and thumped Harry Negus on his dome to get attention. Harry was watching the still-life tableau round the communications post and was glad to be given free speech. He said earnestly, "What I don't understand, Chief, is how she came to rest like that. That is a very cool position to come to rest in. Who is she?"

"We'll never know until she stands up and we can see her face. Just for now, there's work for you. I don't want to monkey with any channels in case that signal gets in again. Just take a look in the Medi-centre and see what goes on there. If Mathias is operational, get him along here."

Carter went round the set straightening limbs and laying out his living dead in greater comfort or decorum, as need was. He had completed the circuit when Koenig groaned briefly and sat up holding his head. He was seeing Alan Carter in double vision, but recognition was no problem.

"Alan?"

"Commander."

"What goes on? No, don't tell me. There was a signal from Pelorus."

Koenig was on hands and knees shaking his head slowly left and right. Still on all fours, he crossed the floor to where Helena Russell was lying with a cushion under her head. He was still seeing double, but to have two was a bonus, either one was food for vision. Taking a middle point his hands homed gently on her shoulders and the physical touch brought a change. She snapped into single focus, hard-edged and slightly numinous but one single figure.

Her eyes opened wide and showed something like panic. Holding her in a firm grip, he said, "Helena. Easy now. It's all right."

The set was coming to life. Main-Mission personnel struggled unsteadily to their feet. Paul Morrow jacked Sandra from the deck and sat her back on her swivel seat. Koenig said sharply, "Don't switch in the long-range probes, Paul. Use the internal net. Call for an all-sections report."

"Check, Commander."

Helena said, "It's all right, John. You can ease off that bone crushing bit. I'm feeling better by the second."

Bob Mathias, second in command of the Medi-centre, was in with a rush followed by a half dozen orderlies with trolleys. With everybody mobile, he was as out of place as a nun at a coven. But he went through the motions. "Casualties, Commander?"

"None here. Wait for the reports though."

All Alpha sections were reporting in. Wherever a communications post had relayed the transmissions from Main Mission there had been the same effect. But, except for a broken arm in Hydroponics, where a technician had fallen awkwardly across a tank, there was no call on Medicare.

As the last report came in, Koenig said, "We can claim we were lucky. Kano, take it slowly and be ready to switch out. Have Computer run an analysis. Clean up and get into working rig. Command conference in ten minutes."

John Koenig looked round the circular table in the command office and saw that the top brass of Moonbase Alpha were out of motley and back on circuit as a working team. It was unbelievable that less than one hour ago they had been on stage in a musical extravaganza.

Starting with Victor Bergman, Koenig said, "Let's have it, Victor. What was all that about?"

"Nothing so mysterious, John. Computer shows two elements. We all heard the rhythmic noise. I'd say it was the carrier. It made us attend to it and try to sort out a pattern. But there was another frequency outside aural range that had an impact which we did not know about until it did its work. The brain is an electrical machine. This frequency was like a jamming device on the higher nerve centres. I leave the medics to say how it worked."

Koenig turned to Helena. Composed and efficient, she said, "That's about it, John. The effect was much the same as an electronic stun beam. No permanent damage. I wouldn't like to say that a very long exposure would be harmless. There's a very delicate area where memory lives and the patterns could be altered or even erased. What the critical time would be is anybody's guess without research on animal subjects."

Koenig said, "So we have a planet, Pelorus, within

range for six days. First reports showed we could live there. Then we get this. What is it? A warning shot? Stay away?"

There was a silence. Sandra Benes said hesitantly, "I think there is something we are forgetting, Commander!"

"Which is?"

"*Our* probes picked up the signal and brought it in. It was not *beamed* at us by a deliberate act."

Alan Carter took it up. "That's a point, Commander. For all we know, they don't know that there is life on this moon. It could be a permanent protective screen that they put out."

"Whether by accident or design it puts long-range assessments out of court."

Bergman said, "That's so, John. But the data we have shows a planet with an atmosphere we can use. How many of those are there? I don't have to remind anybody of the statistics against finding the requirements for human life. Can we let a chance like this go by?"

Koenig stood up and walked to a direct-vision port. Pelorus was a hard, unwinking jewel on the black velvet star map. It could be their future home. He said, "What about the other planet, Copreon?"

Kano had the answer to that one, "No dice, Commander. In the six days we have, it stays on the other side of the sun. Outside extreme Eagle range. It has to be Pelorus."

They were all looking at him. The loneliness of the command slot was once more borne in on Koenig. He could ask for advice, and he got it in good measure, but, in the end, he had to make the choice. He walked back to the table and stood behind his chair. "Since we can't stand off and make a judgement we have to go and look. Position as before except that we go in blind. The same party. But a different Eagle. Alan, take down Eagle Six and bring up an armed craft. Blastoff in twelve hours. Meantime, I'd like you, Victor, to see if you can cook up any kind of pro-

tective screening. Alan got some cover from space-
rig. Any questions?"

There were none. Helena Russell hung back as the
rest filed out. Together, they stood by the direct-
vision port and looked at the distant planet. She said,
"Can you imagine what it would be like, John, to
walk about in sunshine on real grass."

"Hold it. Computer said nothing about grass."

"Grass and water and hills in a blue haze."

"For a scientist you have a romantic streak. Its as
likely to be lichen or desert and lava dykes."

"You don't really believe that?"

"I'll keep an open mind."

"As long as you leave room for hope."

He ran his fingers under the elastic bell of honey
blonde hair. "There's always that!"

A buzz from the communications post made a period. Sandra Benes appeared head and shoulders on
the screen, dark eyes like black milk and wide with
alarm, "Commander!"

Koenig was through to Main Mission at a run. The
big screen had the familiar picture of the moonscape
around Alpha. But there was a change. Marching in
from the horizon was a column of moondust, like a
waterspout that a tornado might pluck out of the surface of a sea. It veered and twisted but maintained a
course. It was set on a line that would take it across
the centre hub of Moonbase Alpha.

CHAPTER TWO

Main-Mission staff watched the big screen as though transfixed by a malevolent eye. Koenig had to speak twice to get attention. "Paul. Controller!"

"Commander?"

"Figures. What speed does it have? How long have we got?"

Paul Morrow kicked himself into action and, once moving, took a count of five to get a printout. He put the text under the screen like a caption and it was clear for all to see.

CENTRE OF VORTEX APPROACHING AT 50 KILOMETRES IN THE HOUR. WILL REACH ALPHA PERIMETER IN 30 MIN-UTES.

Noise was building like the rumble of an oncoming freight train and a tremor could be felt through the deck. The power being generated was immense. They were staked out in the path of a juggernaut.

Koenig did the sum, but asked his question for confirmation. "Victor. What's your assessment? Will the defence screens hold up?"

"No chance, John."

"What's driving it?"

"A massive energy beam could be manipulated to create different pressure levels. Vacuum at the centre. Classic vortex effect. Once moving it could be bowled along."

"Controlled from the planet?"

"We must believe that."

"To warn us off?"

"More than warn us off. When that hits, we'll have no interest."

Koenig hit a stud and klaxons began to sound out. Red telltales winked on in every communications post in the sprawling base. He said, "Red Alert, Paul. I want all personnel in deep shelter. Alan, Victor, with me."

As the three raced for the command office, Paul Morrow's voice began an all-sections call, "Attention all sections Alpha. This is an emergency. All sections shut down. Seal all pressure locks. All personnel proceed to deep-shelter stations. Hurry it along."

Sombre faced, Victor Bergman said heavily, "It's no good, John. We save our people. But for what? How do we feed them with the base in a rubble heap? How do we rebuild?"

"It hasn't happened yet. There's one thing we can try. Meet force with force. Whatever set that up is using a simple physical phenomenon as a weapon. That's something we can fight. Now why didn't they use this beam as a direct threat to Alpha? As I see it, they knew it wouldn't work out. Our antimeteorite screens would hold it off. So the storm effect is all we have to worry about."

Bergman, watching the monitor on the command console, said, "That's good reasoning and you could be right, but the storm's still good enough to do their work."

"Suppose we set small controlled atomic explosions in its path—wouldn't that break it up or deflect it?"

"It's playing with fire in that area. You never know what chain reaction we might start up."

Carter said, "But it's a chance and the best we have. How do we do it, Commander. Eagle Six is still sitting out on the pad."

Koenig was thinking like a machine. "We still have some atomic-blasting devices that were used to excavate waste pits when Alpha was set up to dispose Earth's atomic waste. There's precise data on power, range and fallout. Victor, get a rundown from Computer on the minimum distance from Alpha where we can work without overloading the radiation screens. Meanwhile, Alan, get a detail loading Eagle Six. Fast. Every second pushes the crisis point closer home."

The klaxons stopped, but Red-Alert signals went on. Light levels dropped to emergency systems. Moonbase Alpha was like a ghost town. Main-Mission staff, waiting for the last order to evacuate, watched the monitors and saw Eagle Six jack herself off her launch bed in a flurry of moondust.

On the big screen, the tornado was rolling in and the noise of its passage had notched up to a demonic shriek. Its outer wall had gathered a frenzied mixture of surface trash and small rocks. It was immense, rearing into the star map like a grey cooling tower.

Eagle Six turned across the storm's front and dropped out of sight behind a long lava dyke. Sandra flipped to on-board scanners for a closer picture.

Two bulky figures moved down the landing ramp carrying red drum containers and their slow, deliberate motion was at odds with the nightmare rush of the frantic column. It was the classic dream sequence of impeded flight with the victim shackled and crawling away from a pursuing beast.

Living it, blow by blow, Sandra Benes was leaning tensely over her console. She jerked out, "Faster! Move faster!"

Paul Morrow left his desk and moved uncertainly, ending up behind her chair. They were all projecting their will for the slow moving figures to finish and get back aboard the Eagle. Hands on Sandra's shoulders, Morrow said, "It has to be slow. 'More haste, less speed' was never more true than out there."

The outriders of the freak storm were already send-

ing whirls and eddies of moondust into the long de-
pression. Bergman's voice came up on the Eagle command net. "Eagle Six calling Main Mission."

Tanya had moved over to cover Alan Carter's vacant
desk and answered for Control. "Main Mission. Go
ahead."

"We have two charges set. Time's against us. There
won't be any more. But, as I calculate, the storm centre will pass over this point. Detonation from Main
Mission on 30,050 megacycles. Pinpoint this reference
and set up an automatic detonation sequence. Any
questions?"

Tanya looked across at Morrow. It was bad, but it
was clear. For his money there was every chance that
Eagle Six would still be in the area when the charges
fired. He used his own comlock to break into the
Eagle net.

"Understood, Victor. But for God's sake move it
along and get out."

There was work to put his mind on Red Alert.
"Kano, get Computer to set up a ring diagram with
the charges at centre. Key the storm to a probe and
bring it up as a moving blip. Let's see it up there on
the screen."

Koenig and Carter were jogging deliberately up
the ramp when the screen blanked and Kano's ani-
mated diagram filled the scanner. He had done better than a travelling blob. He had a broad red finger
probing slowly down from top dead centre towards
the trench which lay across the diameter line of his
circle. At the midpoint, there was a green asterisk for
the site of the bomb. Green stood for hope in his
book.

It was neat and impersonal. Morrow linked for instant transmission of the detonating signal when the
red hit the green.

When it was set up, there was a hand's-breadth to
go and only minutes on the clock.

Helena Russell, fresh from the final evacuation of

her Medicentre, rushed in for the end game and
said breathlessly, "Where are they, Paul?"

Koenig's voice answered her.

"Eagle Six to Main Mission."

"Come in Eagle Six."

"Are you set?"

Kano took the reply. "All set, Commander."

"Automated?"

"Automated, Commander."

"Everybody below then."

"We have to bring you through the screens."

"No time. Get below. That's an order. We'll veer
off and come back. Out."

Morrow looked round the circle of faces. The vibrations in Main Mission were shifting small gear
from the desks. The red finger had three centimetres
to go. Nobody wanted out. But the man had said it
and the habits of discipline died hard. He said curtly,
"All functions to fail-safe. Get below."

There was an orderly rush. Last out with Morrow,
Helena Russell saw the gap closed to a centimetre
and the hatch of Main Mission slammed definitively
at her back.

On board the hurrying Eagle, trying to get the
curve of the moon's ragged surface between himself
and the epicentre of the explosion, Koenig watched
the payoff on the miniature scanner. He saw the immense foot of the towering column lip into the dyke
and straddle over to rush on. For a split second he
believed that it had been all in vain and some technical carve-up in Main Mission had wrecked the sequence. Then the moving tower was opening like a
flower in time lapse, growing, spreading and filling
the star map with a surging grey cloud.

There was time for Alan Carter to grin widely
through his visor and give a thumbs-up signal, then
the Eagle was booted up its tail as though by a cosmic foot and the pilot was fighting for sea room to
stay in flight and miss the jagged outcrops of moon-

rock that were lifting to tear at the underbelly of his reeling craft.

Eagle Six would have given sober satisfaction to its distant makers on Earth planet. Prototypes had been engineered for disaster and tested to destruction. This time it was for real. With landing gear ripped away and half the superstructure gone, the bulkheads to the command module held fast and Carter limped on in lopsided flight with a rash of red telltales flickering on his damage-report panel.

Koenig called through to the passenger module, where Bergman was wearily jacking himself off the deck in a welter of broken gear. "Victor? Are you all right?"

The answer came back heavily laced with static, "That has to be a relative term. Pressurisation's gone to hell. If Alan doesn't get down, he'll lose his tail section. But, as against being wholly dead, I'm fine."

Carter said, "I heard that. I'm flying blind, but I'll set her down as soon as I can."

Even as he spoke, the grey dust cloud was thinning out. It was a timely break. Dead ahead, a long cliff of moonrock showed a livid streak where, in time past, the great eccentric machine of Gwent had blown itself into eternity. Balancing his failing craft on two remaining retros, Carter proved for one more time that his place in the top slot of Eagle Command was not up for grabs. Airspeed nudging zero, Eagle Six dropped on the jagged remnants of her undercarriage and the overstretched console flipped to Non Op.

Main-Mission staff, crowded round the emergency command post in the underground bunker, felt the ground at their feet lurch. Regular lighting went out for the seconds it took for relays to trip and bring in minimum replacement on the storage system.

Sandra Benes, face a pale ivory oval in the gloom, looked her question at Morrow. He was already working at the link with the main computer. That patient sentinel, alone in Main Mission, was rattled, but still batting. After a couple of exploratory whirrs it cleared its channels and pumped out a half metre of tape at the distant outfall.

Kano, anxious for his partner, read it off. There was some information about the craft *Voyager One* shaken out of a memory bank and then a series of false starts before the circuits got themselves sorted. Then the message was clear.

FIVEFOLD INCREASE IN RADIATION LEVELS. PERIMETER SCREENS HOLDING. METEORITE DAMAGE IN DORMITORY AREA K. STORM CENTRE DISPERSED.

At the same time, robot trouble-shooters in the power section picked up the loss in the bunker area and switched to an alternative channel. Lights dimmed briefly and went up to full strength.

Meeting Helena's eye, Paul Morrow took a direct line to the Eagle command net and put out a call, "Main Mission calling Eagle Six. Come in Eagle Six."

Up aloft, relays tripped and the signal went out from the empty control centre. There was no answer. Grey clouds of moondust swirled over the complex. Inside and out, it was a dead world.

Helena said, "They saved the base. But for how long? If the Pelorusians can raise one storm, they can raise another. How often can we use atomic charges without passing the danger level for radiation? And where is Eagle Six?"

Sandra said gently, "Try not to worry, Dr. Russell. Alan is the best pilot in the service. He would try to run before the blast. With all the radiation out there, it is not surprising that we cannot receive a signal. When we return to Main Mission, there will be a grid search. Hectare by hectare. We will find them."

"And the sooner we get back up top, the better." Paul Morrow shoved down studs for a full set of communications points in the bunker system. His voice spoke into every gallery and Alphans sitting on long rows of facing seats, as if in a travel tube bound for nowhere, listened to the handout.

"Attention all sections. Eagle Six has been successful. The storm centre has been dispersed. Return to operational sections. Radiation levels must be monitored at all times. Damage-control crew to dormitory area K to check report of meteorite penetration. Move it along and stay alert. We've had two hits from Pelorus—if it is Pelorus acting up; we need to be ready for the third. Out."

Orderly lines of Alphans filed along the corridors. Ragged breaks in the dust cloud could be seen from direct-vision ports. The moonscape was settling back into its age-old pattern of silver-grey sterility. Everything was as it had been, except that three leading hands were on the missing list.

Koenig would have been surprised at the feeling that was being generated in the base. He knew he was generally respected as being an able administrator and one who knew a great deal about space operations, but he knew also that his aloof manner and hardcase stance on the maintenance of good order and a disciplined programme could be misunderstood. But he believed it was part of the command package. He knew of no other way to keep Alpha running as a viable enterprise.

Back in their sections, all personnel waited and listened at communications posts for some news of Eagle Six. They heard Sandra Benes calling repeatedly, "Main Mission to Eagle Six. Do you read me? Come in Eagle Six." It was a tribute to the missing executives that the ongoing threat from Pelorus was forgotten.

Paul Morrow felt the responsibility of decision and had a problem. Eagle Six could be anywhere on a vast quadrant of the moon's surface. Once down in a drift of moondust she would be so camouflaged, that only a lucky strike would pick her out. He could use every available man and machine on a fruitless search and leave Alpha wide open. Something, he had to do.

The best could only be a compromise. He put Tanya on the Eagle command desk and gave her a brief. "Get three reconnaissance Eagles out. R.V. over the West Beacon. Understood?"

"Check, Controller."

"Kano, have Computer work out a search pattern for three craft."

Main Mission slipped into action like a well-oiled machine. He listened to the pilots making procedural checks and turned to Sandra. "I want Pelorus on the screen. Five seconds flat. Beam everything we have down there for data collection. Then out and we'll study what we have."

She could have said, "I hope you know what you're doing,"—but there was something in his tone that stopped her. With a quiet, "Check, Controller," she went to work, sensitive fingers running over the communications console as if with independent life. The big screen blanked, glowed with silver rain and cleared to show Pelorus in a blow-up that filled the space from edge to edge. There was no change except that the picture was bigger than they had seen before. The overall yellow-orange color was intense, relieved by bands of fleecy white. Whatever had been using the Alpha probes to feed in its own disorientating beam had jacked it in. The planet was as warmly inviting as a ripe fruit.

Precisely on the count, Sandra killed the picture and the screen blanked. Kano said slowly, "They tried twice. Each time, we had an answer. They're not to know how near they came to success. Maybe they're waiting for a move from us?"

It could be so. Morrow considered it, trying to put himself in Koenig's place. There was no substitute for going down to take a look, but there could be some very sophisticated opposition down at ground level. But there was time. He could use an hour for a concentrated search for Eagle Six. He said, "Swing the main probes. Back up the search craft. Be ready to cut the signal if there's any infiltration from the planet."

Sandra filled the screen with a moonshot to the horizon on every side and brought in the three Eagles as an inset. It was a silent world with the angular craft drifting like ghosts. On the second sweep, she had it plain. Unexpected, but satisfactory and complete. Koenig's hawk face behind the glinting curve of his visor was superimposed on the moonscape. He was patiently talking to his comlock, knowing that only blind chance would get his signal through the radiation and Alpha's screens. "Eagle Six calling Main Mission. Come in Main Mission."

Helena Russell met him at the hatch of the decontamination chamber as the outrider of a ticker-tape welcome. There was no need for words. Her expressive eyes said it all. Flanked by Carter and Bergman, he walked into Main Mission to a standing ovation.

Sandra, pushing her luck with Helena, moved impulsively from her desk and put her arms round his neck. "You *did it,* Commander. No casualties. They've stopped trying."

Almost roughly, Koenig disengaged himself. He said, "Alan's the one you should thank. He drove the Cannonball. Now for God's sake let's get on. Where are we up to, Paul?"

"Back to square one. We tried a five-second probe. No incoming signal. No further data. The planet looks good."

"Put it up again."

Making up for her off-beat display, Sandra went by the book. "Check, Commander."

Rock steady, Pelorus was centred on the big screen. At this distance, it was a prime piece of real estate waiting for occupation. The question had to be whether the price was right.

Koenig said, "Magnification."

The apricot circle expanded, filled the screen and continued to peel away. Detail was less clear and San-

dra stopped to make a refined tuning ploy. Then it
was in motion again, stretching out every which way
until she hit the limit. "Extreme magnification, Commander."

They had what was plainly a long mountain range
and some dark, irregular patches which could be vegetation. Helena Russell, who had been doing some
checking on her own account, said, "Still no life signs,
John."

Koenig said, "Hold it there, Sandra, and be ready
to cut. What do you make of it, Victor?"

"What are we expecting? Even with that magnification, human artifacts would not show up. Think of
Earth planet from Moonbase Alpha. But we know
there's intelligent life there. Two deliberate attacks
on Alpha spell more than coincidence."

"Intelligent life, but not necessarily human life."

"The life-sign probes are programmed to identify
life patterns like our own. How could it be otherwise? Nobody can anticipate what must be, by defi-
nition, unknowable."

"But the *Voyager-One* data tell us that conditions
equate roughly with those on Earth. Similar life forms
would evolve."

"Not necessarily. Think of the possible permuta-
tions over a million years with two choices at every
evolutionary step. And it isn't a case of two choices,
as Helena will bear out."

Helena left her monitors and joined the group.
"That's right, John. The possibilities are truly infinite.
There could be life which we are not equipped to
recognise as life."

It was nice to have specialists about, but Koenig
reckoned that there was still room for a practical man.
He had been stunned by an electronic signal that
had to have a source and his base had been near to
destruction in the path of an artificially whipped-up
hurricane. Somebody was down there engineering it
and it was somebody who thought near enough like
himself to have a will and a purpose. Communication

must be possible. It came down to a question of whether they should try or whether it was too hard.

He considered the long stint they had done and the many disappointments that had come their way. There was no guarantee that they would ever see a better chance. It had to be checked out.

He said, "I see no reason to change the programme. Get that armed Eagle on the pad, Alan. We'll leave as soon as we have the range. Meanwhile, I suggest we all get some rest. Close down the probes and brief your stand-in team for maximum caution."

When he had them aboard the Eagle and Carter was methodically going through his sequence of preliftoff checks, Koenig had a moment of self-doubt. He was hazarding six of the most experienced personnel of his base. If the mission ran into the ground and they failed to return from Pelorus, it would knock a hole in the command structure. But he told himself that nobody was indispensable. Kano's face on the small scanner reassured him. It would take a lot to throw that same one. He had shifted over to take Paul Morrow's control desk and given his own computer slot to Tanya. Scott Randle, a senior pilot, was in at the Eagle command desk. There was no real problem; it was just his ego out for a prowl.

Randle said, "Eagle Nine clear for blastoff."

Carter's even growl answered, "Eagle Nine to Main Mission. Counting down."

Kano opened a section of the perimeter screen and Eagle Nine lifted in a minor storm of dust and small trash. She hovered, turning to pick up a course and then accelerated away leaving a trail of drifting debris.

In the passenger module, Victor Bergman and Sandra Benes worked at a littered table on a set of six skeletal helmets, fashioned from hoops of stainless-steel conduit. Each was powered by a small cell to rest at the nape of the neck and had a selector dial like a decorative plaque at the forehead. A foam-rubber grummet set in the rim made for a comfortable fit.

As he finished one, Bergman held it up for inspection. Ever tactful, Helena said, "Very nice, Victor. If that doesn't impress the natives, nothing will."

"Try it."

She hinged away her visor and gingerly pulled the contraption over her head. It was a snug fit, lightweight, easy to wear. It gave her a regal, Egyptian look. "How does it work?"

"The selector's at zero. You have nine stops from low to maximum. It's a degaussing effect. Raise the power to counter any disruptive signal beamed your way."

"Suppose it's just an audio signal."

"Earplugs."

Morrow said, "If these Pelorusians have any sense of humour, they'll die laughing."

Sandra said, severely, "If you have a fault, Paul, it's *ingratitude*. We've worked very hard to save your thick head. I don't know why we bothered."

"No offence. Give me your little embroidered handkerchief and I'll wear it in the crown."

Eagle Nine fled on. Moonbase Alpha diminished to a mole on the moon's ravaged cheek. Pelorus was growing as if in a zoom lens. The nudge of a sixth sense told Koenig that every step of the way they were being monitored by some observer who would not show his hand. He used his link with Main Mission. Whoever was watching might as well have something to fill his ear.

"Eagle Nine to Main Mission."

"Come in Eagle Nine."

"Beam a signal to Pelorus, but make it short and take care. Tell them to expect a landing from a peaceful reconnaissance party."

Kano did them proud. His measured, even tones would have brought tears to the eyes of a Sioux war party. He said, "This is Moonbase Alpha calling the people of Pelorus. We are travellers in space. We came from Earth planet. We are peaceful people. We come in peace, seeking a place to make our home. The craft approaching Pelorus carries our leader Commander John Koenig and some of our chief citizens. We ask you to give them a hearing. We ask for your friendship. Please acknowledge."

The transmission ended. Silence flowed in like a tide. The Pelorusians, if they understood, were giving nothing away.

The blank refusal to talk was beginning to irritate Koenig. He thumped the release stud of his harness, shrugged out of the gear and opened the hatch to the passenger module. Leaning in, he said, "What do you make of it, Victor? Is it that they won't answer or is it that they can't?"

"It must be the first. We've seen what they can do. Anybody with that technical know-how, would be able to unscramble a signal."

"Where does that leave us?"

"Your guess is as good as mine, John. But it has to be on the negative side. Nobody's saying welcome."

Eagle Nine took a sheer turn that had Koenig grabbing the hatch coaming for support. Carter called sharply, "Commander!" and Koenig whipped back to the co-pilot seat.

The long instrument spread was going crazy. Every dial was in a frenetic spin and the on-board computer was throwing out course data that would have had the Eagle disappearing up its own tail.

Kano had started a rerun of his friendly, neighbourhood moon talk and a persistent, hammering crackle drowned it out. At the same time Koenig felt a familiar pounding in his temples and a wave of nausea. He hauled himself out of his seat and made the passenger hatch at a stumbling run.

"Headset! Try it out!"

Bergman was already there to meet him and settled a tubular helmet on his head. For a second the effect was worse and then Koenig got a hand to the control and brought the power up to match. It was incredible.

His brain went from confusion to crystal clarity. Only Carter was still unprotected and Eagle Nine was flinging herself about like a demented gnat.

Koenig said, "Fix him up for God's sake!" and clawed his way to the co-pilot squab. Switching control to his own panel, he cut computer links and took the control on manual. Eagle Nine steadied to even flight and Koenig brought her round on a course with the planet surface dead ahead and filling his direct-vision port.

Sandra Benes, virtually sitting on Carter, had fixed his headset and was tuning his muddled head. Her personal pollen cloud, pleasantly laced with sandalwood, was a disturbing element in itself.

Prodding at him with a slim forefinger she said, "Alan! You're not trying. Say when!"

"If I say that, you'll go away and I'm just getting to like it."

She fended herself off and joined Bergman at the hatch. All watched the planet surface. There was a change in colour. Although there was still an overall hue of yellow orange it was much less strong and other colours were coming into the composition.

Bergman answered the unspoken question. "It's an atmosphere trace. Seen from a distance, it looks all of a piece. But down at ground level, it's probably hardly noticed."

Carter had been watching his instrument spread. "It's steadying, Commander. I have readings."

It was true. Eagle Nine's computer was back in business. They had a working ship. But there was no signal from Main Mission to say that Kano was still talking.

Koenig flipped to transmit. "Eagle Nine to Alpha. Come in Alpha."

There was no reply. He tried again. "Eagle Nine to Alpha. Do you read me? Come in Alpha."

The communications executive, earning her keep, said, "We have passed through a layer of strong magnetic fields. This could blanket our signals. Perhaps

signals from Alpha have not reached Pelorus at all.
That is why there has been no answer."

Koenig said, "Let's hope you're right, Sandra. It still
doesn't explain two unprovoked attacks. But I'll give
them a local call."

Far below was the long humpback of a chain of hills
set in a flat plain which could be a sea or a prairie
feature. There was still no sign that human hands had
gone to work to engineer the environment for their
own purposes.

Koenig said, "Greetings to the people of Pelorus.
This is Commander John Koenig of Moonbase Alpha.
We come in peace and ask for permission to land and
to meet you. Let us know your thoughts."

Helena Russell and Paul Morrow had crowded into
the command module. The six Alphans were stock still.
The bland surface of the planet gave nothing back.
Helena said, "It's no use, John. They just don't want
to know."

"Then we'll have to pick our own spot to land and
go find them. One orbit, Alan, and then go for a
planetfall."

Eagle Nine ran from bright day into a spectacular
sunset and bore on into black night with a star map of
huge stars fixed like chips of orange diamond. Earth's
roving moon was a bland new feature now showing a
brilliant orange yellow through the atmosphere filter.
Down below, there was nothing to see. If Pelorus
boasted any urban centres, they operated a curfew.
There was no sign of man-made light.

There was the glint and fret of a long run of a wine-
dark sea, hills clothed with vegetation showing black
in the low lumen count, empty plains. It was to all
intents a virgin planet.

Dawn met them with long bars of rose madder and
pale viridian and held them fixed to the direct-
observation ports in awe and admiration. Pictorially,
they had gotten themselves a winner out of the cosmic
hat. Helena Russell, leaning over Koenig's chair back,

breathed warmly in his ear, "It's a beautiful planet, John."

"Handsome is as handsome does. I'll tell better after twenty-four hours on the surface."

Carter said, "Where, Commander? Where shall I put her down?"

They were crossing a gently undulating plain, evenly coloured auburn like a Pre-Raphaelite head. Carter dropped to zero height and cut back forward speed until they were drifting slowly over the surface and Bergman could make a judgement. Using a short-range scanner set up in the passenger module he brought the plant carpet, life size, to his table. It was hair fine, coiled and springy. It fitted no description in his catalogue of Earth-type flora. But it looked A-Okay for holding a picnic on the grass. Nature's own mohair run.

He said, "It looks good. I need samples. If we have time, I'd like to stop and take a look. But, clearly, we need to search for centres of occupation if they exist."

Sandra had been running a check on the atmosphere. She said, "There is breathable air. Slightly oxygen rich. Pressure like Earth's at four hundred metres. Gravity less than Earth's. Temperature twenty-two Celsius."

Paul Morrow said, "It all adds up to an idyllic set. You'll be bounding about like some spring lamb."

Helena said thoughtfully, "Now there's a thing . . ."

Morrow, recognising a lack of courtesy, added, "And, of course, you too, Helena. Two spring lambs."

But it was pure science that was troubling the medical wing. She said, "Conditions seem right for life. But where is it? We haven't seen any animals. No birds. No herds grazing on what looks like a natural habitat."

In the command module, Koenig had come to a decision. He said, "Set her down, Alan. Anywhere here. We'll make some surface checks."

Eagle Nine drifted down like a feather, flexed gently on her jacks and the motors cut. Carter looked sharply at his co-pilot. It was one thing having the over-all commander as a helper, but he liked to be captain in his own ship. Koenig had not moved. Getting it straight he said, "Did you switch off, Commander?"

"No."

A puzzled man, Alan Carter ran through a firing sequence. There was no joy. The motors stayed dead.

Koenig said, "Hold it."

Belatedly, the auto trouble-shooter had come up with a signal. He read it off. "Panel K43. Gone diss. Blown by overload."

"What overload?"

"That's what the computer says."

"No problem, but it's a bastard to get at. I'll be an hour. It's under the tail decking."

"Inside or outside?"

"Easier to reach from outside."

"Then we'd better get at it. The tourists can take a walk on the veldt."

The long-range probes swung from their random

CHAPTER THREE

Eagle Nine's landing ramp dropped to the oval of scorched earth, blasted clear of lichen by the flare of her rocket motors. Out of spacegear, but still wearing Bergman's patent degaussing helmets, the six Alphans reached ground level and looked about. It was incredible to be freely in the open, without life-support systems, under the vast bowl of a real sky with a sun standing over the horizon like a bright apricot penny and a tangible movement of warm air against their faces.

Helena Russell had a sampling kit on a shoulder strap. First things first, she wanted a rundown on the local variant of grass. She knelt at the edge of the oval and opened her satchel. At close quarters, the lichen was seen to be about ten centimetres deep, curled like human hair, with filaments a fraction of a millimetre in diameter that were springing individually from the surface of the earth.

She snapped off a single strand and laid it along the back of her hand. Her startled cry brought Koenig to her side at a run.

"What is it, Helena?"

An angry red line marked the site of the strand of lichen. "The grass, John! Tell the others they mustn't touch it. It's like an acid burn."

Koenig hurried her inside and watched her neat economical movements as she worked on her hand at the medical desk. He said, "I'm sorry."

"Sorry for what? It's a nothing."

"Sorry for your disappointment. Pelorus looked good. I wanted to bring you to a world we could make a life in. All there is out there is a sea of acid."

"It's out there somewhere, John. We'll find it."

Paul Morrow's shout from the outfield made a period. "Commander!"

Head and shoulders out of the hatch, Koenig saw his group at the edge of the clearing. There was no need to ask what was o'clock. The area of the oval was already significantly smaller. The lichen was already showing another feature. Its regenerative capacity was plainly enormous. It was slowly pushing in to win back the lost ground. Helena's abandoned pack was already just inside the auburn tide. It was settling slowly like any sand castle as the acid ate into its fabric.

Carter said, "Holy Cow! Only look at that. What will it do to Eagle Nine?"

The question hung about with no good answer coming up. All eyes tracked round to Koenig. The faint plume of blue gas rising from the half-consumed pack tripped a relay in his computer. He unshipped a fire-fighting canister from the bulkhead of the passenger module and pitched it out for Carter to catch. "Try foam."

Bergman said, "Good thinking, John. There's an alkaline base. It could work."

Grey foam jetted from the nozzle with a hiss. Carter threw a metre-square blanket around the pack and stood back. For ten seconds there was a digestive pause. Then the lichen erupted.

A quick spasm of heat drove at exposed hands and faces. Morrow had Sandra by the waist and was throwing her back; a column of blue-green flame flared higher than the ship. When it sank away as quickly as it had come, there was a blackened patch the shape of the foam blanket eaten out of the warm brown carpet.

Alan Carter, dusting ash off his chest said, "That

does it, Commander. It gives us the time we need to fix the fault and get the hell out of here."

Calculations were racing through Koenig's head. The man could be right. But it would be a one-off exercise. If for any reason Eagle Nine was still nailed to the pad at the end of the hour, there would be no repeat performance. They would be staked out for a slow, but certain, death. Not all that slow either, the way the lichen reproduced itself.

The only sure way was to move Eagle Nine to a better site. Ducking back inside he fished out his binoculars and then climbed up the superstructure to wedge himself on cross members of the ship's girder spine. They had come down close to the foothills of a long mountainous feature that closed the horizon to the north. If the motors had not jacked in, it would have been the next obvious step to taxi over and take a look.

The first slant of rising ground was barely two kilometres distant. It was clear rock or baked earth with no visible vegetation of any kind. It rose to a flat plateau which in turn ran back to a mountain face with a deep overhang. All in all, it had the appearance of a vast quarry, though detail was obscured by the angle of vision.

He knew for a truth it was a better bet. He said, "Break out the halftracks. We'll tow the ship out of this crap. Use foam dispensers to clear a path. Then we know we can make the repair we need."

All hands worked at it. Without power to drop the equipment on a freight loader, it was a physical chore to manhandle the small, but heavy, halftrack excursion trolleys out of store and down to ground level. When it was done and tow lines fixed, Carter and Morrow used manual worm gear to lift Eagle Nine off of her flat plate feet and drop her massive wheels. Stripped to the waist in the rising heat, they worked against a narrowing time gap with the lichen a metre from their feet when all was done.

Koenig had the halftracks in line abreast taking the

strain and ready to go. He walked forward with Bergman beside him, both carrying canisters, and they sprayed out a narrow carpet of foam. They counted five and sprinted back to the cover of the trolleys' curved transparent windshields.

Carter and Morrow heaved themselves onto the leading plate feet, Sandra and Helena prepared to shove in the forward drive. With more area carpeted with foam, the explosive ignition, when it came, rocked the chore buggies on their tracks and temperature gauges surged momentarily to eighty Celsius. Then the way was clear and the clumsy caravan was jolting ahead.

Carter clambered round the angular frame to get into his pilot seat. It occurred to him that any sudden stops by the halftracks would have Eagle Nine bearing down on their backs. Sitting up front, he was well placed to see the action and reckoned soberly that for a primitive piece of horse-and-cart technology it was working very well.

As soon as the tracks bit, Koenig and Bergman were out again and going ahead to the limit of the cleared ground. They shoved out another tongue of foam and beat it back to a safe distance. It was gruelling work. But it was progress. If supplies of foam held out and the human operators blew no personal fuses, it was in the bag.

Morrow dropped from his perch and went forward to relieve Bergman. Alan Carter heaved him into the command module and gave him the braking drill. Then he too went forward to give Koenig a spell. Working it three ways with two operating and one drawing breath, they crept on without a check. Behind them, a charred wake slowly healed and was covered again by the bland auburn lichen as though they had never passed.

Stripped to the waist, streaked with sweat and greasy ash, the three front-runners fell into a rhythm of total effort. For Koenig's money, as he took a spell on Helena's halftrack, it would be all one and welcome if

Pelorus went into spasm and disintegrated into atomic trash.

Helena, on the footplate, was totally committed to steering a course. There was a single joystick. Forward to feed power equally to both tracks, left or right for differential speed. It made the small, powerful buggy highly manoeuvrable. But it could spin on a dime and the hint of a careless shift would have them boring across into her partner with the tow lines in a snarl.

As a doctor, she could judge that they were forcing a physical rate that no human frame could keep up. She said, "One more stint, John, and I'm calling a halt. Sandra and I will spray round and hold it back, while you take a break. That's official."

Koenig wiped sweat out of his eyes with the back of his hand and stared ahead. Carter and Morrow had pulled back. There was the thump of one more explosion as a long ribbon of lichen hit the flash point. As the column of flame died away, there was a change in the scene ahead. He steadied himself against the shockwave, hanging on to the transverse hoop that separated the operations platform from the freight deck of the halftrack. A long incline of grey-green rock, smooth as a billiard table was lifting out of the auburn plain.

Carter waited for them to pass and swung himself aboard. When he could speak, he said, "That's it, Commander. Home and dry. As fast as you like, Helena."

Motors dropped to a growl as the dead weight of Eagle Nine lumbered onto the incline. Koenig was out of programme and Helena waved across to Sandra to go on for a full due and make for level ground on the plateau.

Bergman saw it first and was thumping the direct-vision port to get attention. But three of the five down below were wrapped in a private world of exhaustion and the other two were concentrating on the way ahead. From his lofty perch, Bergman was seeing the first visual evidence that had come their way that some life form had been up and about on Pelorus. The long ramp of rock opened to a level floor set like an oval tarn in the flank of the hill. Blind chance could never have levelled it off. It had all the earmarks of a prepared landing ground. To prove that it was so, the face of the cliff dead ahead, under the overhang which screened it from view from above, was developed like the facade of a tower block.

The halftracks lipped over the brow of the ramp and drove on until the Eagle was on level ground. Working in concert, Sandra and Helena killed the motors and Bergman, brought back to duty with a jolt, heaved on a manual brake.

Half a kilometre away, windows in the bas-relief caught the sun. The scale was humanoid. Koenig said, "I guess we need to clean up. If there's anybody home, they know we're here. This is the programme. All hands back up Alan to clear the fault. Without power, we have no defences. When the ship's fixed, we can go in with the argument of a laser to back up diplomacy. Let's go to work."

If there were any observers in the rock-bound tower, they gave no sign. At a time when only Alan Carter could work in the confined limits of the compartment under the tail section, Koenig used binoculars for a close scan of the frontage. No interested row of heads, humanoid or otherwise, lined the windows to watch the visitors.

He passed the glasses to Helena Russell. After a long silence, she said, "Allowing for technical differences, it's like Petra."

"Petra?"

"In Jordan, isn't it? The rose-red city of the Nabataeans. Once a big centre for caravan routes. Then it was a lost city for over a thousand years until it was rediscovered in the nineteenth century."

"This isn't rose red."

"No. Cut out of rock, I mean. This Petra was a kind of hidden city, only reached through a network of narrow ravines. They had everything, temples, tombs, houses, a big theatre. All cut out of solid rock."

Koenig recognised that in spite of their recent past on Alpha, there was a lot about Helena Russell that he knew nothing about. He said, "That interests you?"

"Surely it interests me. I guess if I hadn't opted for medicine, I'd have wanted to do archaeology. It's the same thing in one way."

"How?"

"Trying to find out what makes people tick. You look back over the years and strip away all the technological trappings and see what basic needs people have and how they organised themselves to meet them."

"The lowest common denominator."

"You can think of it like that, but I like to see the highest common factor."

"The realist and the optimist."

"It's not being an optimist. You can't practice medicine and stay starry-eyed."

"You just look starry-eyed most of the time."

"A compliment. If it *is* a compliment. I don't often get them from you. It must be this mellow light."

Sandra Benes swung herself lithely through the hatch. "Commander. Alan says he's all set for a trial run. He'll leave the bay open until he's sure."

Koenig settled himself in the pilot chair and went deliberately through the preignition checks. Eagle Nine fired sweet as a nut. From a collection of scrap metal, she was back on stream as a viable strike craft. He said formally, "My compliments to Captain Carter. Tell him to close the lid and come aboard."

To Helena he said, "Ask Paul to prepare the half-tracks for loading. I'll drop the freight hoist."

With all hands aboard and crowding into the command module, Eagle Nine trundled forward over the arena to within fifty metres of the rock face. Seen close, the frontage of the tower block was impressive. At ground level, there was a terrace tiled with hexagonal green slabs and a long canopy at the height of the first floor.

Koenig gave protocol a last fling. Using 1420, he sent out a call on the ship's transmitter and at the same time shoved it out on a repeater from the cone. His voice reverberated hollowly from the enclosing cliffs.

"This is Commander John Koenig. We come from the moon which has appeared in your gravisphere. We come in peace and goodwill. We are seeking a place to live. We will do nothing without your help and co-operation. We await your answer."

He ceased. "Your answer. Your answer," echoed in from the external pickups. Like latter-day Petra, they had gotten a ghost town.

Carter said, "Maybe a laser beam through the front door would stir them up. We owe them that for what they tried to do to Alpha."

Bergman said slowly, "It isn't possible that they wouldn't show an interest. I don't believe there's anybody there. But now we know there has been occupation. There must be other centres and one or more must be still operating. We could look elsewhere."

Morrow said, "But time's not on our side. We saw nothing in one orbit. No cities. No signs of life. That isn't conclusive, but do we have time to make an extensive search? And, for that matter, do we still want to know? If that lichen's typical vegetation, it's no good. Graze a cow on that and you'd have the shortest legged ruminant in agricultural history."

Koenig said, "I think I have to agree with that. But having come this far, we can't leave without trying to contact the people. Also, they might continue their attacks on Alpha. We have to put our case and get them to hold their hand while we drift clear. First of all, we'll look inside this building and see if it tells us anything. For this trip, Alan, stay aboard with a watching brief. We'll keep in touch on the half-hour every hour. Ration packs. Side arms. Stick with these fancy helmets. Spruce up in case we meet their president."

Helena and Sandra exchanged glances. Helena said, "Now he tells us. There isn't so much as a yellow ribbon in the stores."

The shore party assembled on the apron and Carter retracted the ramp. He lined up the main armament to fire over their heads and took a firing grip in either hand. The Alphans crossed the gap and reached the terrace. Koenig set the pace, neither slow, which might mean that they expected trouble, nor fast, which might be interpreted as a threat.

It was all strictly for the absent birds. Nothing moved. Ground level was sealed by long transparent screens that felt like glass to the touch. Inside, the centre section could well have been a big reception lobby. There was a long desk over left, with a free-standing wall feature behind it made up of yellow uprights and pale green shelving. There was none of the detritus about that would point to a sudden evacuation. All evidence of occupation was swept bare and tidied away. Walls were uniform in fluted cladding, coloured dove grey.

The only decorative feature was a long frieze on the right-hand wall, which was difficult to see at this angle, but looked like a full-colour job of people and places. There were some stone settles, low backed, missing the soft furnishing that might once have made them comfortable. Paul Morrow hammered the glass with a balled fist. There was no obvious way to get inside.

Koenig flipped open his comlock. "Alan. Do you read me?"

Carter's face appeared in the palm of his hand. "Loud and clear, Commander."

"We'll move aside. Line up on where I am now. A short burst. Not too much power. We have to break a way through."

"Check, Commander."

Koenig drew them away beyond the next support

pillar. There was a crackling hiss and a thread of eye-aching light jetted from below the Eagle's cone. A white asterisk flowered briefly on the glass. Then the whole panel shivered and became opaque as it was crazed by a million hair-fracture lines.

At the point of impact, there was a fist-sized hole and air gushed from the interior in a long exhalation.

After all the years spent in medicentres, it carried a familiar bouquet to Helena Russell's sensitive nose. It was clinical, aseptic, slightly tinged with formaldehyde. Whatever else, the Pelorusian outpost was germ free.

Koenig enlarged the hole, tapping around with the butt of his handgun. The glass had shivered into splinter-free nodules about the size of walnuts. With a half-metre wide panel clear, Koenig edged through, laser on first pressure. Bergman followed, Paul Morrow brought up the rear with a valedictory wave to the watcher in the Eagle.

They stood in a row facing the frieze. It ran the whole length of the wall, a good thirty metres. Brilliantly coloured and as fresh as the day it was painted, it set out a slice of everyday life for a humanoid species not greatly different in physical type from the Minoans of ancient Crete.

They walked the length of it in silence, each one absorbed in the detail of an alien culture. There was a highly mechanised farm spread with domed silos and a control tower. A long moving gantry ran on shuttle-shaped feet along two metal rails. Below it was a strip of cultivated land. Clearly, they had gotten well past the days of grubbing about with a hoe or a digging stick. The food chain was all buttoned up with nobody in sight to test the grain with a spatulate thumb and cast an eye on the weather.

It was the same tale with a still from factory life. Rows of sleek machines spun thread from hoppers of green candy floss, passed it to weaving frames, stretched it, dyed it, turned it out in a stack of bales from deep indigo to tomato red.

The time saved by all the automation seemed to be spent in pleasures of the flesh. Two thirds of the long record was devoted to a spirited search for ways and means to tap joy at its root.

As a medico with varied practice and an insight into the wilder shores of the human, it seemed frank, but not surprising to Helena Russell. If anything, it pointed to areas of similarity in culture patterns between these aliens and their distant cousins on Earth planet. Except that on Earth the scene might have been featured by Hieronymus Bosch as a terrible warning of actions likely to lead to hell fire. There would have been a frieze of demons waiting to punish the revellers. Here, it was clearly A-Okay and as good a way as the next to get through three score years and ten. If you could stand the pace.

It showed plainly enough that on the physiological plane, at least, evolution had come up with the same answers to vision, locomotion, the principle of the opposed thumb and reproduction of the species. Paul Morrow said, "They'd like a print of this in the pilot's duty room. Save all the sweat of working a rota. They'd all be on standby."

It earned him a slow burn from Sandra Benes, who was a simple girl at heart and took the view that sex was a private exercise between two interested parties. She said, "I think it's all a big turnoff. And for that matter, if you look at their faces, it's all very sad. They've left themselves with nothing else to do and the artist who painted it has understood that."

Morrow put an arm round her shoulders, taking care not to be misunderstood, and said slowly, "I think you have the right of it, Sandra. I don't think our working community in Alpha would fit there too well."

Interest in the frieze had made them insensitive to aural clues. The whine of a motor and the faint rattle of some power drive was well over the threshold before Koenig got the message and whipped round with his laser ready to fire.

The noise came from an open-ended corridor beyond the reception desk and they waited in a line, backs to the pictorial strip.

The noise was in the room itself. There was nothing to see. The source point was moving steadily behind the rear wall of the reception desk. All heads turned slowly as they tracked it along. It could have been a mechanical rat.

When it finally appeared in the open on a straight course for the broken window, it was revealed as a squat, metre high, mobile bollard with a revolving receptor dome glowing a nice shade of purple. It was mounted on a square plinth with black, caterpillar tracks and had flexible antennae coiled in loops and hooked tidily on storage cleats.

Morrow, on Koenig's left, had taken first pressure and was prepared to go to work on the military principle: "If it moves shoot it."

Koenig's hand clamped on Paul's wrist. The move was either not seen by the robot can, or was discounted as not concerned with the job in hand. It rolled on until it was positioned in front of the broken pane. Antennae uncurled themselves from store and felt delicately around the frame. The purple dome turned green for thought and there was a metallic mutter as it talked busily to itself and passed data into a memory bank.

Once satisfied that it had it right, it spun neatly on its tracks and began to withdraw. It was the ultimate in a maintenance crew. No chatting up the householder about who threw that vase then? No worried shake of the head and a beef about glass prices and how it would be a one-off job and the account would be subject to an inflation clause. It was off to draw a piece from store and get it fixed before the autumn leaves blew in.

Koenig signed for the others to follow. It was a lead. Maybe somewhere in the back rooms there was a janitor who could answer a few questions.

The corridor was tiled like the reception area and lit by white ceiling ports. The bollard trundled itself along to an intersection, turned right like a parade-drill instructor and moved into another open area with a choice of three elevators set in the facing wall. Two were small and a pictograph on the lintel made it clear they were intended for a maximum load of six persons. The six stylised human figures were three male and three female. Equality could go no further. Morrow said admiringly, "You have to hand it to them. They never miss a trick."

The right-hand opening was much larger and was marked up with the picture of a forklift truck. It was the freight hoist and the bollard rolled into it as of right.

Koenig made a decision. "It isn't interested in us. We'll go with it. Otherwise we wouldn't know when to get off."

One disadvantage was plain when the hatch sliced shut. Freight, having no feelings, got no light. Except for the corpse glow of the purple dome, which turned flesh to a tortured El Greco tint, there was nothing to see by.

The cage dropped. Bergman counted to himself. Not intended for personnel, deceleration was savage. By the time they had sorted themselves out of a confused heap, the hatch was open and the bollard was on its way.

Bergman said, "Five seconds. I'd say we're down all of fifty metres."

The bollard had almost reached journey's end. They were in a huge, natural cavern. The floor had been levelled, true, but the walls were rough-hewn. Lights slung on gantries disappeared into the distance. Storage bays, coded for reference by winking light panels, lined the sides. Robot workers of all shapes and sizes stood around waiting for the good word to swing into action and make any repair required up top.

Sandra said, "Where have they all gone? Where are all the people?"

The questions hung about unanswered. The only movement was from their guide who had gone along the line to a control point and plugged himself in to

tell his tale. It triggered a reaction down the line. A
glazing detail swung itself into action. A small convoy,
led by a bollard with a yellow dome, made for the
elevator landing. There was a purpose-built carrier
holding a new glass unit and two backup bollards
with specialist tools and a coil of sealing strip.

Bergman, who had accepted all the details along
with the principle of an automated repair service, had
wandered off through a connecting arch to another
part of the forest. His voice came to them in a muffled shout. "Through here! This could lead somewhere."

They found him standing beside a long silver shuttle
suspended on a monorail set below the roof. There
was a platform with stone seats like the settles in reception. Lights were still burning in roof ports. It was
clean and tidy and, except for any software, looked
all ready for the next commuter rush.

Koenig said, "I don't come anywhere near to understanding what goes on. What do you make of it,
Victor?"

Victor Bergman ticked points off on his fingers,
"Item: Whoever built this place intended to go on using
it. Item: The withdrawal was planned and orderly.
Item: They set it up so that it would be in working
order when they wanted to use it again. Item: They're
so advanced that communications would be no problem. If they wanted to talk to us, here or on Alpha,
I'd say they could do it."

Paul Morrow took up the count. "Item: They don't
want to know and they tried to destroy Alpha."

It was like a game, but Sandra put her finger on
the key question that stopped it dead. As a communications expert she was used to having somebody at
the other end of the channel. "Item: Where are they
and are they watching us?"

Koenig walked to the front of the shuttle, found a
stud beside the entry hatch and shoved it down. The
panel slid away. He said, "This goes somewhere.
Maybe their main centre is at the other end of the
line. Having come this far, we should check it out."

He looked at his time disc. "Time to call Alan. See if you can raise him, Sandra."

It was not easy and the picture, when she had it on the miniature screen of her comlock, was distorted, giving Alan Carter a maniacal lopsided twist. "Commander to Eagle Nine. Do you read me?"

"Eagle Nine to Commander, strength two. Go ahead, slowly."

Koenig took the comlock. "Anything going on, Alan?"

"Not a thing. Except that some bean cans have started fixing that glass."

"We're still searching. Stand by."

"Check, Commander."

The five Alphans climbed aboard the shuttle and Bergman, earning his keep as scientific adviser, sat himself at the operating console. The switchgear was minimal. He had a choice of two controls. There was a red knobbed lever with left-to-right movement in a narrow slot. It was pushed over to the far right where there was a pictograph of a shuttle at rest at a platform like the one where they were. The other had a green grab handle and moved in a slot at right angles to the first one. There were five marked positions. The centre option was marked with a zero and the lever was set there. Above it, the two stops had yellow symbols; below were the same symbols in the same order but coloured red.

Thinking aloud, with his balding head thrust forward in a characteristic pose, Bergman said, "It moves. It has to stop. It has to go forward or backward. One of these is a brake or a holding device. One regulates speed and direction. So the red one has to be the brake. It could also switch on the power. Then a natural move would be to shove the other lever up and forward to move off. Are we sure we want to go?"

Koenig said, "We have to try to find who's behind the attacks on Alpha. We have to convince them that we're no threat and get them to hold off. Surely we have to go."

Bergman slid the red knobbed lever over left for a full due. A low humming filled the car and settled to a quiet, powerful throb. Lights came on from ceiling ports. There was a definitive click from the hatch as it locked itself. Some forward thinker had decided that there should be safeguards against absent-minded citizens trying to leave at an unscheduled stop.

The engineer shoved the green handle to its first yellow stop. The shuttle took off smoothly along its rail, accelerating to a ceiling around twenty kilometres in the hour and holding rock steady to that. It was enough to be going on with. There was time to look about and see where they were going.

In fact, there was not a lot to see. The plain walls of the underground depot had not been exploited for commercial gain. The pleasure seeking Pelorusians had other fish to fry. At the end of the platform, the line branched two ways with a choice of two tunnel exits. There was no demand on the driver. The shuttle took the left-hand hole and plunged into the darkness of the pit.

Koenig left his seat and walked about the car. It would seat thirty-two on double seats, eight on either side of a central aisle. There were contoured headrests, small parcel racks and a freight bay in the rumble. It was neat, functional and efficient. Except for the unexplained attacks on Alpha, there was every reason to think well of the people who had designed it. He completed his tour and sat down beside Bergman.

"How does it work, Victor?"

Linear motors, without a doubt. Stator and rotor parallel instead of coaxial. It's something I recommended when Alpha was in construction. It's cheap and foolproof to operate."

"But costly to set up. That's what killed it. Here they must have surplus production to burn."

Helena Russell said, "How does that square with

the frieze upstairs? You wouldn't rate those people as technologists?"

Koenig said, "Art and life don't necessarily match up. Somebody had the know-how and you don't get it by sleight of hand. There has to be training and hard work. Then there's another factor that creeps in. People get to like the work for its own sake. They might start out thinking that when they've built their Xanadu they'll sit back and enjoy it; but it doesn't work out like that. The acts of working and planning alter them. They can't be idle."

Helena said, "You have a point. *Two* points. The art work could be wish fulfillment. It could be the very opposite to the way they are. If they've hived off all the chores to mechanical wonders, they might well have an elitist society where everybody is an intellectual. I'm not sure that it would be healthy in the long term."

Leaning forward between the head stalls, Sandra Benes listened to the conversation, watching one and then the other like a tennis umpire. Picking up the break, she said, "There's another thing. If one generation makes everything *perfect,* the next generation has nothing to do unless it breaks it all up and starts over. Both the picture and the technology could exist together."

Paul Morrow pulled her back into her seat. He said, "Give me a little of your attention. We don't often get to ride on the Metro. Sing little European songs in my ear as if we were going for a day in the country."

"I'd be a fool to go on a trip with a chauvinist pig."

"There is no better companion on a ramble."

Whatever reply she would have made was forever lost. The shuttle had steamed into new territory. The tunnel was white tiled and brilliantly lit. The walls funnelled out into the huge dome of another cavern. This one was clearly a more important centre and might well be the hub of a network. There were shuttles standing at other platforms and a line of spares in a siding waiting to come into service. There was an island in the centre, reached by many flyovers, with a circular kiosk under a linear display panel which could only be a clock. It was still working. As they watched, the symbols changed and one of them was identical with the first symbol on Bergman's control panel.

He had brought the lever back to zero and the shuttle moved gently to a stop. He shoved over the brake. Lights dimmed and the hatch clicked again. There was a sense of journey's end. But there was no busy work party rolling out a red carpet.

There was progress of a kind. As they stepped out to the platform, a P.A. system cracked into life and an even, metallic voice made an announcement.

"Fastabelindo in vra katika an devasto. Praeli. Antrenda in lamen."

It ceased. Paul Morrow said courteously, "And I wish you the same."

Koenig spotted a row of elevators. There was one with the cage in position and the hatch open. He said, "We'll go up and take a look. If there's nothing, we rejoin Alan and get back."

When all were in, he selected a stud and shoved it home. The hatch sliced shut. The cage began to move. A fine mist of tiny violet droplets fell from the roof and Helena's alarmed, "John!" was the only word spoken. Her recognition that there was a general anaesthetic out and about was too late by a couple of seconds. Koenig tried to grab for her and they fell together to a soft foam floor as the elevator surged on up the shaft.

CHAPTER FOUR

John Koenig rejoined the world of sense as quickly and unexpectedly as he had left it. His brain was suddenly at a stretch and trying to see all the angles, but he made no move to advertise the fact.

As far as physical comfort went, he was, anyway, ahead. The floor he was lying on was carpeted with a soft pile. His head was chocked on a pneumatic pillow which was rising and falling gently at a comfortable human tempo. The only sound was a muted syphonic gurgle, which told him that his headstall was part and parcel of a human creature who had missed out on lunch and could do with a refuelling session.

He opened his eyes and found he was looking over the pleasant contours of Helena Russell's chest at the underside of her chin. Beyond her head was a grey fluted wall. At the edge of vision, he could see the outline of something that might be a desk or a table.

Moving a centimetre at a time, he checked his belt. His comlock was still there. And his laser. Thinking it out so that he knew to a fraction what moves he was going to make, he gathered himself together and mobilised every erg of his motor for a smooth turn and rise.

Koenig was on one knee with his laser searching about for a target. He felt a sense of anticlimax. There was nobody about except the five Alphans.

They were in a quiet room maybe ten metres square. Walls were uniformly grey with no visible entrance.

There was a single, oval lighting port in the centre of the roof. They had a table, which was set with bowls of unfamiliar fruits, goblets and a couple of carafes. Chairs with blue and yellow cushions were dotted about. There was a long settle against one wall. Lying every which way, his four companions were stretched out on the deck.

Even as he checked out the set, there was movement. Paul Morrow sat up and said, "Sandra?"

Koenig said, "Right beside you. She's all right."

"Commander? What goes on?"

"You'd need a crystal ball to answer that. We walked right into it."

Helena Russell sighed deeply, sat forward and shook her head, sending a shock wave through her hair. "John?"

"The same."

Medical training died hard. She went on, "That's a very efficient drug. Instant action. Complete anaesthesia. No side effect."

"You're supposed to say, 'Where am I?' Where's your sense of occasion?"

"Okay, where am I?"

"Your guess is as good as mine."

"Sometimes, John Koenig, you're a very disappointing man. What's the use of giving the right cue, if you don't have the right answer?"

Sandra played it by the book. Paul Morrow had picked her up to fix her on a couple of cushions. Dark eyes suddenly wide and enormous, she said, "Where am I?" and wrapped her arms round his neck.

"With me."

"That's nice."

She closed her eyes and relaxed, then opened them suddenly, as total recall flooded in, and struggled to get on her own two feet.

Last to join, Victor Bergman heaved himself slowly to his feet. He said, "Could it be that they knew from the first which way we'd go? Left us to our own devices, knowing that we'd see the shuttle, knowing that we'd follow our noses?"

Koenig's thinking had been along the same line, but he couldn't accept it. "I don't see how. They weren't to know we'd crack the glass and trail the repair detail. But I'll concede that they could have had us monitored along the way. It wouldn't take long to set up the trap in the only route we could use to leave the cellar."

Helena said, "We keep saying 'they,' but I can't see those people in the frieze behind this kind of cat-and-mouse game. Or behind the attacks on Alpha, for that matter."

Koenig said, "Who then?"

As if on cue, a section of the wall sliced open and a voice, using English slowly, as though its owner had to think out each word from semantic principles, said, "That is correct. You are correct in that. The humans do not have the will or the power to take action. The direction of affairs on Pelorus has passed to us. We have the knowledge and the power. We are the masters now."

It came from a tall figure standing foursquare in the aperture, though where precisely the sound had its point of origin was hard to say. The head was a bland ovoid, finely tooled with microgrooving, so that, as the point of vision of a watcher altered, there was the impression of features. Then, as the eye steadied to a particular point, there was only the plain smooth surface.

It was a curious and disturbing effect, though the rest of the body shell was no more than a superbly cast model of a well proportioned male figure, carried out in what could be stainless steel. High on the left of the chest, was an oblong ID plaque with letter symbols.

The voice went on, "You will come with me. The Council of Pelorus will question you."

Koenig said, "Suppose we say we refuse?"

"That would be unreasonable. Why should you act in an irrational way?"

Koenig's laser was lined up on the android's dome and he had taken first pressure. Helena's hand on his arm checked him. "John. They must know we can't do anything against them. Wait. We should hear what they have to say."

Koenig shook his head as if to clear it. It was uncharacteristic of him to shoot first and talk afterwards. He said shortly, "Of course, we should do that. Keep a check on these degaussing helmets. Be ready to counter any mind-bending effects that might be going about."

To the visitor, he said, "Very well then. Lead and we will follow. We have questions of our own to ask."

Outside the door, they were on a circular landing. In the centre was a single elevator in a translucent shaft. Clearly, they had been moved to another part of the complex. The guide walked straight in and waited. With a shrug, Koenig followed.

It was a short trip and they emerged in natural daylight with the familiar warm tinge of the Pelorusian atmosphere. There was glass all around and views of rising, mountainous peaks in every direction. They had come out to a penthouse feature on a tall building set in tourist country.

Their guide crossed a lobby dotted with exotic plants in white tubs and a glass patio door slid away at his touch. They followed him through into what was clearly an executive suite with panoramic views on all sides and a ceiling that was in continuous flux with slow spreading patches of changing colour.

Koenig suddenly knew for a truth that the ten androids sitting round the circular green table, still as metal castings, were using services that had been set up by somebody else. They were going through the motions. They were imitating a procedure that had been devised by men.

Seen closer, there were differences in the androids. Eight had a stainless-steel finish like the messenger.

Two, sitting side by side, were pale gold. One male, one female, taken perhaps from some perfect, classical mould, throwbacks in form, at least, to a time even before the world of the frieze.

The left-hand marker of the golden pair turned his eyeless, ovoid head to watch them in and, although the voice which began to speak was difficult to place, it seemed to key with his actions and he was the likely source.

"You have been brought before the Council of Pelorus to give an account of yourselves."

For Koenig it was the last twist of the knife. If he had indeed finally gotten to meet the mechanical genius which had masterminded the attacks on Alpha and had rejected any attempt to go for two-way communication, he reckoned there were explanations due to him. Mastering his anger, he went for a cold, biting exposition. He said, "I am John Koenig, Commander of Moonbase Alpha. But you know that. Since you have listened on the Alpha net long enough to know the basics of our language, you also know that our mission is peaceful. But, without warning, you attacked our base and attempted to destroy us. You must answer for that. Why do you treat us as enemies?"

The site of the voice shifted and altered in timbre. This time it was the female android. "You *are* enemies."

Helena Russell said indignantly, "How can you say that? You know nothing about us. Certainly, we are looking for a place to live. But we are not thieves. We would negotiate. We offer our skills and the knowledge of our race in return. You have acted like barbarians."

The first speaker raised a shining metallic arm. The discussion was getting out of control. Instead of a hand there was a ball fitment from the wrist and a crablike pincer with a jointed thumb acting against a flexible plate. But the gesture was wholly human. If he had had a gavel he would have been pounding the table top. He said, "Enough. The Council of Pelorus does not have to justify itself. You are here. That is enough. Your asteroid platform has penetrated into our space and our calculations show that already it is upsetting the physical laws which have always operated here. You are unstable, biological creatures. We have no intention of allowing you to bring your unresolved problems to this planet, which is now a place of order and good government."

Koenig could have said that there was no place more neat and tidy than a mausoleum. But he stuck to his main point. "That is no explanation. We tried to communicate with you. You refused."

"This Council does not have to explain itself to creatures such as you. How could you understand the interplay of pure intelligence, freed from the interplay of human selfishness and folly? The question is what now is to be done with you."

Koenig's laser was in his hand and his voice was hard edged. "We are not defenceless. Perhaps even pure intelligence has enough self-interest to want to stay in being. There is no progress in this meeting. We are leaving now to return to our ship."

There was no move from any one of the Council. Koenig said, "All right. We'll find our own way out."

Morrow, nearest the door, kept the messenger in his sights and backed slowly off. He was a metre short of the hatch when he was brought to a stop. Watching him out of the tail of his eye, Koenig saw him feeling with his free hand for the object that had suddenly appeared in his path. Clearly, it was there to touch; but there was nothing to see.

Sandra Benes, two paces to the left, was using both hands and seemed to be running them over the surface of an invisible wall. She said, "It's no use, Commander. There's a barrier."

Koenig tried the head man. "So you have some technical tricks. Release us!"

"No."

"I'll count five and then drill some holes in that fancy head."

"That is a typical human reaction to a problem. It is easy to see which of us is the barbarian."

Koenig said, "Stop me when it moves, Sandra," and began to count, "Five . . . four . . . three . . . two . . . one." There was no response from Sandra Benes who was still shoving away like any method actor miming frustration.

Following the sequence in strict time, Koenig called, "Zero" and fired as he spoke. Paul Morrow hit the same split second with a backup reaction. Two fine beams flared from the lasers and converged towards the same target.

It was an illuminated diagram and the beams should have homed in the same square millimetre on the android's bland forehead. But there was no joy. The combined strike was held off, ten centimetres off target, in a white asterisk of intense light.

Bergman said quickly, "Save it, John. It's no use. They left us the lasers because they know they have protection. It's an incredible force field."

Koenig's arm fell to his side. It was one thing to be outsmarted by a human adversary, but to have to cry uncle to a tin wonder gave a shrewd knock to his spirit. It was no help to feel that he was in some sense to blame. It was his own decision that had brought the reconnaissance team down on Pelorus. After all the experience on Alpha's troubled odyssey, he should have known better. If anything, he should have come in strength, with a squadron of armed Eagles, and blasted a path to a conference chamber.

Seeing that his position as a negotiator had been badly undermined, Helena Russell tried a different tack. "Listen. We have both used force and failed. But you must agree that you taught us its use. You tried to destroy Alpha. It cannot matter to you whether we are here or there. Allow us to return. Our moon is travelling on. Soon it will be out of your gravisphere. Before it passes out of sight, we should exchange what knowledge we have. That is how intelligent people should behave."

One feature of pure intelligence in action was plain enough when the android spoke again. There was no harmonic of triumph or satisfaction in winning the hand. A move had been made and that move had been countered. It was a mathematical exercise with no winners or losers. He had missed being turned into scrap metal by a fraction, but his voice was unaltered. "Your arguments all have the same base. You are anxious to preserve your lives a little longer, though it would be clear, to an intelligent life form, that there is no point in such concern. The statistical likelihood of your finding a place to live is too small to have significance. Here, or on your moon, you are doomed. It is only a question of sooner or later. We, on the other hand, live forever. The future, the past and the present are all one. We exist unchanged. We are not misled by the changing pressures and needs of an inefficient, biological, life-support system."

Bergman said, "But you were created by man in his own image. Originally, you were programmed by biological men. You could not have existed as you are without men, however independent you have become. Does that not make you pause to consider whether we have not something to offer?"

"That is the first profound thing that has been said. It is still typically egotistical, however. Travellers like yourselves should know that nothing is impossible. It is unlikely that a thinking machine could be created without the evolution of a biological form. But it is not impossible. In this case, you are right. We have a tie with a human culture. Not on this planet, but on the planet of Copreon. There are a thousand of us on Pelorus. Over the long millennia of the indefinite future, we shall perfect ourselves. Pure mind, uncluttered by emotions or fears or restless appetites. I will tell you my name. I am Gregor. I am President of the Council. Each at this table has a special area of responsibility. Power. Defence. Research. Supply. My consort, the Co-President, is Zenobia and she has charge of all aspects of communication."

Sandra Benes, having a professional interest, said bitterly, "It's a great pity she did not use her skills to better effect."

It was unlike her and Morrow said, "For God's sake, Sandra, try to make friends. Get her views on Koch resistance and polarized, electrolytic capacitors. Give her a quick burst of Algol. Make her love you like some sister."

If Zenobia had been listening, she made no sign. Gregor, however, once having broken into free speech, seemed anxious to get the record straight. He said, "What is creation? What makes a living person? In the end it must be put down to blind chance. Simple elements come together and increase in complexity. Once that has happened, there may be an emergent quality which could not have been foreseen."

To prove that all Alphans were not trigger-happy and could follow a catalytic concept down a hole, Helena Russell said, "There's some truth there, in the last bit, at least. Think about water. Two gases combine and produce a liquid. Who would think, looking at them, that the product would be so different. You wouldn't expect the *wetness* of water for a start. That would be a new thing."

Privately, Paul Morrow reckoned she was going a bit far and Gregor might think she was taking a subtle swipe at the qualities of his refined mind. But, in fact, it got a good press. The other golden oldie, Zenobia, said, "Precisely. I have often said that the judgement of the female mind was greater than the male."

Gregor swivelled his head to look at her and lifted his crab claw for hush. "You will understand what I say, then. Though you are quite incapable of appreciating the full extent of the change that took place. We too are from Copreon and we built the community infrastructures which you see. But not, at that stage, for ourselves. There were others here. Copreons. Clever in their way, but reaching a state of degeneration as biological communities always do in the end. The environment of Pelorus was dangerous to them and accelerated the speed of their decline. For us, it was an ideal situation. There are infinitely complex magnetic fields here and sources of immense power which can be tapped. The android cortex was able to make use of these forces. This was the new factor, the catalyst, if you like, which moved the android community on, from its simple role as a work force to a positive and independent life with charge of its own destiny and development."

Bergman said, "The laws of evolution operate in a random way. An organism adapts to the environment it finds itself in. So far, our claims to life are equal. But we are not denying you the right to life or the ownership of this planet. Why are you so afraid?"

Zenobia said, "You choose your words badly. The concept of fear is one we recognise in men like yourselves. We can analyse its causes and the actions it produces. But it is an emotion. We do not operate in that area. Dr. Russell will understand me if I say that there is no *affective* side to our mental composition. We have *cognition* and will. What we know, we can organise and this we do. We know that it would be dangerous to allow you to return to Alpha. You will stay here, since you have not profited from clear warnings to stay away."

Choking on it, Koenig said, *"Warnings?* You attempted to destroy Alpha!"

It could have started the seminar off on a second round. Gregor said, "Enough. We have other matters to discuss. This has taken too much time already. You will return to your room. If you resist, it will be the worse for you. Go now."

Koenig turned away as though he was going along with it, and the others, taking their cue from him faced round towards the door. Still turning, Koenig was off to a sprint start round the table. If high-level technology had no chance, there might yet be a place for old-fashioned brute force and ignorance. He aimed to get round behind Gregor and take him apart with his bare hands. For that matter, the original designers of the android body shell must have left some visible switch-gear to cut off their power in case of malfunction.

The ideas were racing through his computer as he gunned round the circle. Certainly, the move had taken the androids by surprise. There was no protective wall to stop him. He was behind the leader, taking in the detail of the smooth metal back. No dice for a visible console. There was a round cover plate between the shoulders with a slot to take a tool. A clip fit. Prised out with a claw. Too long.

The messenger android had stirred itself from its spectator role and was pounding down on him. Koenig grabbed for Gregor's smooth head with the intention of twisting it off of its stalk. Needles of intense pain stabbed from his fingers and seared up his arms. In his mind, he had a flash picture of his nerve structure suddenly becoming glowing and white hot. He was an illuminated man with a cage of bright wires tightening in his throat.

If it went any further than that, he knew nothing of it. Black night filled his eyes. He was out on his feet before the attendant plucked him away from his target and lifted him in one easy swing over its head, balancing him like a rag doll.

What Zenobia had said about emotion was given a practical illustration. Gregor was unmoved. Helena Russell's alarmed cry, "John! What have you done to him?," was countered by his even tones saying, "Return to your room. This discussion is finished."

Helena was trying to reach Koenig, but a wall had dropped to bar her way. Her appeal was agonised, "Let me go to him!"

Gregor was not going to say another word. He had lost interest. Zenobia said, "You must see that he brought it on himself. But I will tell you that he has suffered no permanent harm. He will recover. Now, show that you have some understanding and return to your room."

John Koenig came back on stream with a hard-edged, eidetic image of Gregor's back etched on his

retina and went right ahead with his arrested programme to grab and hold. Textures were all wrong.
He had gotten flesh and a swath of fine hair that came
near to clogging his intake.

Sandra Benes's startled "Eek," penetrated his dazed
head and he relaxed his bone-crushing grip. It was all
very confusing and he was ready to blame Gregor for
working a cunning shift.

Sandra had been leaning over him to take a turn at
the medical chore of soothing his forehead with a damp
cloth and when she could draw breath, she said,
"There's more in this medical business than meets the
eye. I think I shall stay with communications. Your
patient, Dr. Russell."

Helena pushed him back on his cushions. "Take it
slowly, John. How do you feel?"

"Better all the time and wholly tired of being on
the losing end."

Missing the backup services of a fully equipped
medicentre, she went through a series of checks as old
as medicine itself. Pulse was firm and steady at seventy-
four. Head on his chest, she listened to the regular
thump of his heart. Since it was handily placed, he
ran his fingers through her hair.

He said, "There's something to be said for old-
fashioned methods. Stay where you are, I like it."

Reassured, she got to her feet. Basic responses were
A-Okay. "What happened to you, then?"

"It was like grabbing a live power cable." He
looked at his hands. They were unmarked. "Very high
voltage and a tiny current. I guess it was enough to
beat a path along nerve circuits. One thing's for sure.
Unless we can switch them to Non Op, we can't get
near these zombies."

Bergman said, "We tried to raise Alan. No dice.
There's heavy screening."

Koenig swung his legs off the couch and stood up.
He asked Helena, "Can we drink the water?"

"I think so. It's not possible to be sure without
laboratory tests, but as far as I can tell, it's all right."

She filled a goblet and handed it to him and took a bright green fruit, the size of an apple and held it out. "These are good. A bit like mango. Very filling and sustaining."

The flesh was yellow and tasted of yesterday's custard, but she was right on the main count, it was very satisfying. He said, "This is fresh fruit. It must be local grown. So not all the surface is acid lichen and mountain."

Bergman said, "Unless there's a deep-freeze store. The original humans would carry an emergency stock. The androids don't need it, so it's there for visitors."

Koenig went on another tack. "You were all watching the route when we came back here. Any observations?"

Morrow said, "It was quick, like the trip up. Nothing to see. The council meets in a penthouse suite. I'd say this was the admin silo for the human operators."

"They came from Copreon, the man said. Why, for instance? And why wasn't there a backup operation mounted from the home planet to get them out of it, when things turned sour?"

Bergman said, "Could it have been a penal colony? Botany Bay? Maybe they wrote it off or stopped sending their rejects."

It could have developed into a long debate. Koenig walked over to the table and thumped it with a balled fist. He got attention from all hands. "Listen. What's getting into us? We seem to be *accepting* the situation. Let's get things clear. Pelorus is no good for Alpha. Right? Time isn't on our side? Right? There's only one thing we should be talking about and that's getting back to Eagle Nine and getting the hell out of it. Take things one at a time. How do we get out of here?"

They could have said, "You tell us," but they recognised that he had a point. Sandra did say defensively, "We have been *looking*, Commander. But there is no way."

"Take a wall each. Go over every square centimetre. There has to be a ventilation duct somewhere."

They went to work; animals in a strange cage scrabbling around for a way out. Koenig checked the floor area, heaving the furniture aside and knocking every tile with the butt of his laser for any change of note. The table itself was a fixture, standing on a white circular column like a flattened toadstool. On hands and knees he went methodically round it.

Victor Bergman said, "There's a hair crack round the door panel. It can't move either way unless its pulled out or sunk in. If we could force it back . . ."

Koenig lifted his head to hear the broadcast and rapped it smartly on the underside of the table. It did nothing to improve his temper. He hauled himself to his feet and fairly snapped out, "What are we waiting for then? Use the settle as a ram."

Backed to the opposite wall the three men had a seven-meter clear run from the leading end of the ram to the notional door. Koenig said, "Helena, Sandra, one either side. Watch for a movement; shove the panel out of line if you can. Decide which way you're going to move it or we'll all be in a bugger's muddle."

Sandra's expressive eyes met Helena's with womanly sympathy. The top hand was showing a coarse streak. To show him the way to get goodwill and co-operation, she said formally, "Shall I push towards you, Dr. Russell, or will you push towards me?"

"I don't mind."

Morrow said, "For God's sake, Sandra, stop clowning about. This things weighs a ton. Keep your head out of the way or we'll crack it like an addled egg."

Koenig counted down and shoved off from the rear wall with a total mobilisation of every fraction of urge he could get from his motor. The thud of impact, when it came, sent a quiver through the whole fabric of the room and the translucent cover of the ceiling port burst from its catch and swung down on a hinge. The shock jarred Koenig's arms to the shoulder and the heavy settle was out of control and falling to the deck. He yelled "Get clear" and lost his footing.

Morrow had plucked Sandra out of danger by a nanosecond and was flat on his back with the communications expert sitting on his chest. Bergman had tripped over his legs and was picking himself up from the corner. Helena, still batting and with both palms pushing at the panel, said, "We did it, John! It's moved!"

Koenig clawed himself over the wreck of the settle to get to her side. She was the soul of truth. The impact had depressed the panel against some system of holding springs and the lateral shove had wedged it behind the line of cladding. There was a hand's-breadth gap. They were making progress. But from somewhere overhead there was an urgent bleep on orchestral "A." An alarm had been triggered.

Morrow had rolled clear of his elegant burden and joined Koenig at the breach. Fingers hooked in the gap, they hauled away against the inertia of machinery set to keep the seals on. When they had half a metre of free space, Koenig gritted out, "For God's sake, move it along. Out."

Once through, Bergman wrenched off the broken end of the settle and wedged it in the gap. Koenig said, "Now you, Paul."

Without the extra power, the material of the wedge creaked and began to deform. Koenig had to squeeze to get himself through and as he was hauled free, the closing gear developed full power and the moving edge sliced through the obstacle.

Morrow said, "They take a chance with their doors. Anybody hanging about could get himself cut off in his prime."

Koenig said, "Search about. There has to be another way down. They can't believe the elevator service never fails."

Sandra Benes found it and when she had it she was incredulous. There was a semicircular extension on the left side of the elevator trunk. She had released a section of cladding and hinged it open. "Here, Commander. But, surely, this can't be all?"

It was no more than a conduit carrying heavy cables clewed to its walls and a line of handle grabs going down into far distance.

Victor Bergman said, "One thing, John, I don't see an android getting down there."

There was a slight vibration through the housing. A cage was on the way. Koenig said, "Get inside and start moving down. Paul. Then Sandra. Victor. Helena. Make it quick."

Beside the elevator trunk was a small console with a selector panel. He treated it to a long burst of laser fire and saw it glow white hot. It retained its overall shape, but he reckoned any circuitry under the hood would be in spasm. Ear to the shaft, he listened. There was no sound. The oncoming cage had stopped. Last in the conduit, he pulled the curved panel back in place. There was a dim light from small inspection lamps set every fifty metres. The tube plunged down as though it had no end and would finally make out in the mantle of the planet.

Koenig counted two hundred grabs and reckoned they had dropped all of a hundred metres. He called down, "Hold it there." There was an inspection lamp close to his head and he could see the outline of a hinged panel. Making no noise at all, he worked open the inside catch and pushed the door open a crack. There was not a lot to see. From the restricted viewpoint, it appeared to be a landing much like the one they had left. He opened wider and two things happened at once. Below the lower edge he saw the heels of two metal feet and the door itself hit a stop.

Reaction times tried and tested, in a service where a nanosecond one way or the other could mean disaster, he was acting on a gut message that sidetracked his computer. Grabbing for the hold-fast over his head, he jackknifed with both feet together and slammed into the partly open door.

The surge of back pressure came near to dislo-

cating every bone in his back but the door opened for
a full due and he could see the android struggling to
stay upright as the gyro stabilisers in his legs raced
into overload.

Koenig used the purchase he had to swing his own
legs over the coaming and project himself out of the
trap. The android's back was plain to see and the
plate as he remembered it on Gregor. Tearing his laser
from its clip, he stabbed with the finger guard into
the small recess and the plate flipped open. There was
no time to sort out the switchgear. He fired once and
had to sidestep as the tin man dropped like a felled
chimney.

Helena Russell's head was looking over the coaming, eyes full of alarm. Koenig knelt down, panting
like a dog. He said, "Tell them to come out. We need
a break."

Bergman and Morrow turned the android until
they could see its back. The controls had fused in a
lump but there was a bright tag on the inside of the
cover plate with a a legend in the unfamiliar char-
acters and the pictograph of a mine shaft with
branching tunnels.

Although out of programme, there was still movement inside the torso as the power pack continued to
deliver. The head began to turn from side to side.

Hand to her mouth, Sandra said, "It's horrible.
It's like a wounded man."

Koenig was looking for information. He picked a
spot on the back of the head and fired a short burst.
This time there was no force field to deflect the beam.
The metal boiled and opened in a ragged hole.

But the android's locomotory mechanisms went
solo. With jerky unco-ordinated movements it struggled to its feet. Arms flailing, head wagging, it was off
on a random journey that drove it along the lobby
to a floor-to-ceiling window that sealed off one end.

It was three hundred kilograms of metal, shoved
along by legs pumping up and down like pistons.
The glass hardly checked it. There was a character-

istic scatter of nodule fragments, a man-sized hole and fresh air wafting in. The thud of its arrival at ground level was almost instantaneous.

Bergman, as surprised as the next man, was still a mathematician at heart. He said, "That's close. Not more than ten metres. We're at ground level."

CHAPTER FIVE

Other calculations were racing through Koenig's personal computer as he leaned out into natural sunlight and looked at the ground below. He was trying to judge how far they had come on the shuttle and the best guess he could make was round the five kilometre mark. That was straight through the heart of the mountain. Overland would be longer. But surely not more than ten? They could do it in two hours at a forced march and be outside the direct control of Gregor's technical network.

Down below, the android was in a state of smash. It had fallen on a flagged terrace and its own weight had settled the business. The head had rolled clear of the trunk and one leg was broken off at the knee. Instead of blood, it had spilled out a spreading pool of black oil and a litter of small gear.

The face of the building beside the observation window was arranged in courses, with projecting bands every metre, to gladden a rock-climber's heart. It was easy.

The building itself was set in another valley feature surrounded by hills. Below the terrace was what had once been an ornamental garden, now overgrown and neglected. A short scramble beyond the end of the garden, there was an old surface road which had been cut into the flank of the mountain and followed the curve of the valley out of sight in either direction.

Koenig said, "This is our way. Over the hill. Keep it moving."

The android had taken out most of the glass and Koenig kicked away enough for a clear path to the stonework. Each step down was double the interval of the grabs in the conduit, but the ledges were almost ten centimetres deep. He went down smoothly without a check and watched Helena Russell's neat, economical action as she followed.

Bergman was slower, but came down steadily. Paul Morrow was having trouble with Sandra. She was saying, "I *know* I didn't bother in that tunnel, but it was *different*. There was a wall all round. I'm not good about heights."

"Get on or I'll throw you over the edge."

"Commander Koenig wouldn't say that."

"By this time, he'd have thrown you over the edge."

Neurotic as a flea, she forced herself half a metre from the sill and stopped.

"Now what?"

"I can't move. I've gone rigid."

Morrow followed her, held on with one hand and one foot and swung himself round her until her body was between him and the wall. Shifting a swath of black hair with his nose, he licked the back of her neck. "Did I ever tell you, you have skin like that monumental alabaster."

"Probably, and I want it in one piece."

"You can't fall."

"Now we can both fall."

"Left hand down. Then your right foot."

It was slow, but it was progress. Koenig climbed back to meet them and they talked her down. At ground level, eyes almost all pupil, she was full of apologies. "I'm sorry. That height bit was the one piece of space training I had a problem with. Given a little time I can think myself into it, but coming unexpectedly, I get thrown."

Koenig said, "Not to worry. Everybody has some hang-up. Let's go."

They were not too soon. As they reached the edge
of the terrace, a section of a ground-floor patio door
sliced open and a couple of androids thumped, flat-
footed, into the sunlight. They were new models, coal
black, with one arm adapted as a kind of carbine.
There was the hornet whine of an old-fashioned shell
going overhead and the splat of another hitting the
stone baluster and digging itself a pit.

There was good cover in the garden and the
Alphans used it, zigzagging in and out of mazelike
paths towards the boundary. Another half dozen androids had lumbered out onto the terrace. Two stayed
at the balustrade, the rest began to climb over to join
the two who had already reached ground level in the
garden.

From the first minute, when he had begun the
move, Koenig had seen that the difficult bit would be
where cover ran out. Seen close, the rock-strewn slope
to the road above was maybe fifty metres long.
Climbing it, they would be staked out for target practice.

The androids were strung out like a line of beaters,
taking it slow and steady. Overhead, the two on the
terrace were firing at intervals, kicking up spurts of
dust and rock chippings from the hillside. Koenig's
voice left no leeway for argument. He said, "Victor,
Helena, Sandra, make for the road. Weave about.
Paul, with me."

He did not wait to see them move off. Stooping to
get cover from an ornamental wall, he was running
for a half-ruined gazebo back up the track. It had six
square columns supporting a pagoda roof and was
overfull of bright purple vegetation.

Morrow was a half pace behind him as Koenig
vaulted the enclosing rail. They took a pillar each
and could command a view up the garden to the terrace.

Koenig rested his laser on the crook of his arm
and made a marksman's job of it. The range was on
the limit for effective fire. But the bright thread seared

away and licked into the centre of the left-hand android's ovoid head. For a brief count, there was no change and the android sent another two rounds from its carbine arm to whine overhead.

Paul Morrow started navel high on the right-hand marker and slowly shifted the beam to the column of the throat. The searchers were twenty-five metres off, black shadows behind fronds of leaf and creeper.

It was time to go. Koenig took one more shot, picking the chest cavity and the area where a man would have his heart. At ground level, an android broke cover, nearer than he expected and swinging its carbine for a target. Movement at the pillar caught its sensors and a shot thudded into the stonework starting a long fissure.

Morrow took it from the angle, irradiating its head in a white glare. It missed its stride, stopped with one knee raised and rocked wildly as one stabiliser fought to balance the weight.

Koenig signalled for out and they ran back the way they had come.

The party on the hill were scrabbling on all fours in sliding scree. Shots from the terrace had stopped. Koenig shoved his laser in its clip and went up at a run, arms out like a high-wire artist.

Helena was over the rim and leaned out to give Bergman a hand. He was almost done, face a mask of sweat, breathing hard and laboured. Morrow caught up with Sandra, hooked his fingers in her belt and fairly heaved her up the last five metres like a comely sack.

Koenig, last across, took a racing scan over the set and yelled "Flat down!" He threw himself beside Helena, one arm across her shoulders and sorted out what he had seen from memory.

The two on the terrace had gone spare. One was folded over the balustrade and the other was jigging up and down on its springs. The other five had reached journey's end and had a clear view up the hill. It was all Lombard Street to a china orange that they hadn't a hope of climbing it. But they could rake the road with fire and even as Koenig worked it out, a ragged fusillade rattled overhead and brought down a shower of fragmented rock and bright slivers of metal from the hillside.

Koenig whispered to Helena, "Keep flat and make like a snake. We can't stay here."

Shots were still coming, but only from two carbines. There was the scuff and slide of rubble as the rest of the posse tried to climb. Classic tactics. Fire, cover and movement. They had been programmed from some military textbook.

Koenig crawled fifty metres, forcing himself along until every bone ached with the hammering of the rough road. The others came up and stopped, faces streaked with sweat and dust. The sun was almost vertical overhead and the rock surface was hot to the touch. He edged over to the low coping stone that made a continuous rim and cautiously lifted his head.

The black androids were still trying to beat a path up the hill. Over on the terrace, two shining steel androids were looking out over the garden. Top management had come to take charge. Koenig looked at his time disc. There was no saying what snags lay ahead. They should push on. He said, "On your feet and as fast as you like for two minutes."

They could have beaten a drum or played a bagpipe. Nobody seemed to take any notice. When they stopped to lean on the hillside and draw breath, the distant terrace was empty. The failed cliff climbers could be seen moving in single file through the garden. Gregor had called off the chase.

Victor Bergman, when he could speak, said, "I don't like it, John. I didn't believe they would give up so easy. What will they do?"

It was a good question and there were no good answers about. Koenig zipped out of his tunic top, batted a cloud of white dust out of it and hung it over one shoulder. He said, "I'll feel better when I get inside Eagle Nine. Try Alan again, Sandra."

Sandra was already stripped down to a lime-green leotard that could have been sprayed on with a paint gun. She dug her comlock out of her bundle of gear and went through the routine as if she had been sitting at her communications desk in Main Mission. "Commander to Eagle Nine. Come in Eagle Nine."

The small screen was hatched with silver rain. There was no answer.

"Commander to Eagle Nine. Do you read me? Come in Eagle Nine."

She looked miserable. "I am sorry, Commander. There is no answer. But there will be heavy screening here. I have noticed that the mountain is veined with a metallic ore. We are very much enclosed by it."

"Leave it then. Let's get on."

It was a good half hour by the clock before they rounded a bluff that took them out of sight of Gregor's towering admin silo. Ahead of them, the road rose slowly to cross a high ridge through a saddle. Much of the way, there was a sheer drop on the left and, in parts, the road was suspended on cantilever beams socketed in the living rock. It was impressive engineering and another facet to the character of the pleasure-seeking Copreons, if they indeed had built it.

Whoever had built it had not used it for some decades. No routine maintenance had been carried on. They went in single file over a twenty-metre stretch where the roadway was reduced to a metre wide ledge littered with small rocks. Surprisingly, Sandra took it in her stride. She had seen it coming and had talked herself into a positive mental set. Further on, there was another one, this time more serious. Koenig had his party out in a line, holding hands and edging along four fingers of ledge with their faces flat to the rock.

When they were across, he knelt on the jagged

edge of the road and looked at the break. Bergman joined him. "Are you thinking what I'm thinking, John?"

"No accident?"

"That's right. Too even. It was cut across at right angles and then cut away a section at a time. You can see the tool marks."

The others were taking a spell with their backs to the hillside. Paul Morrow said, "So Gregor knew what he was doing. He calculated we'd pass this point beore his goons could catch up. They wouldn't get across there with their flat feet. He hasn't given up, he's gone another way to work."

It was only too likely. Koenig could see a task force going through the mountain to attack Eagle Nine. He said shortly, "Time is against us. Push up the pace."

If they had come to it fresh, it would have been a gruelling trek. It had been designed for power transports which would have ground up the pass in low gear. On foot, in a baking heat that was knocking forty Celsius and already low on physical reserves, they were turning in longer times for every hundred metres.

Victor Bergman was flagging. Face pale and mouth set like a trap he was driving himself on, but Helena was not deceived. She caught up with Koenig who had gotten ten paces ahead of the column. She said quietly, "John, I'm worried about Victor. You know what he's like. He won't complain. He'll just go on until he drops."

Tired himself, Koenig had to kick his brain into making a decision. He had programmed himself to go on until he ran out of road or blundered into the Eagle. He could split the party or hold together and go slow. Finally he said, "All right. Take a spell. Five minutes. I'm hoping when we reach the saddle, it'll be easier."

They lay stretched out flat, getting maximum rest. Nobody spoke. Many stops like that and Koenig knew there would be one when he would never get them on their feet. He timed it to the second and stood up.

Paul Morrow stirred Sandra with the toe of his boot. "On your feet, Pavlova."

"No."

"Get up or I'll kick your ribs in."

"You would, too. You're *sadistic*."

"Think of ice clinking in a glass on Eagle Nine."

She was on her feet with an heroic spurt of energy. "There you see. A carrot is better than a whip."

"For a donkey."

Ignoring him, she walked on to join Helena. Within minutes, it was as though they had never stopped and they were stupid with the never-ending chore of setting one foot after another in a mind-bending haze of heat and pain.

Koenig was a hundred metres ahead when he crested the last steep rise and met level ground. Ahead, through a short defile, there was a bright V of sky and a sense that they had reached the roof of the world.

Stubbornly, he pushed himself on. There was nothing to see until he was at the very end of the pass. Then he looked down at a change of scene that was almost too much to take in. The road curved down along two sides of an oblong box canyon. Towards ground level the cliff sides were honeycombed with black openings that could have been natural caves or primitive mine workings. The floor of the valley was a mass of vegetation, towering cycads, ferns, regular patches that could be under cultivation. At the far end was a clear, flat area of grey rock that would serve as a landing ground.

Koenig unclipped his comlock, dialled the Eagle command frequency and talked to it, his tongue feeling thick and awkward in his mouth. "Commander to Eagle Nine. Do you read me? Come in Eagle Nine."

When Alan Carter's face appeared clear and precise on the miniature screen, he could hardly believe he had it.

"Alan?"

"Commander? You had me worried. Where are you?"

"Any contact with Alpha?"

"Not a whisper. There's a radio blanket on."

"We can't be far away. I'd guess over the hill you can see dead ahead. But I'll put up a homing signal. There's a lush looking valley and a strip you can land on. We'll make towards it and expect to see you. All right?"

"Check, Commander. No problem. I'll be on my way in under a minute."

"See you. Out."

Gaunt and functional, Eagle Nine could make no claim to beauty, but when her bulbous cone lifted over the rocky sky line, she was as welcome as a bird of paradise in full colour. They were making better time down the long side with only a dog leg to the home straight.

Alan Carter came in with a roar that reverberated through the valley and set her down on her jacks in the centre of the pad.

Helena Russell grabbed Koenig's arm and pointed. "Look, John, by that clump of purple bushes."

The noise had brought a small herd out of cover, startled and racing in a compact bunch to get farther away from the point of origin. They were dappled grey and red, about the size of an okapi. Within seconds they were gone, melding into the multicoloured backdrop. But it was a sign of life. Pelorus seemed less sterile.

Carter had lowered a landing ramp and walked down it, looking towards them and raising a fist in what could be a thumbs-up signal.

Koenig had a moment's doubt. If he had been playing it, he would have held fast in the pilot seat,

ranging round with his scanner and one hand on the
firing handle of the lasers. But there was no other
sign of movement. Except for the disappearing herd,
they had the valley to themselves.

Koenig called his chief pilot, buzzing him on the
comlock link and could see Carter stop in his tracks
to answer.

"Commander to Eagle Nine."

"Commander?"

"What did you see coming in?"

"Nothing new, Commander. It's a double range, in
fact, between here and where we first landed. All
bare rock. Nothing stirring."

"Anything at the tower site?"

"Some gnomes fixed the glass. I could see you
follow the first one out. As I pulled out there was
some action. Black android types making towards
the window."

"Hatchet men. If any show, blast them first and
ask questions later."

"Check, Commander."

Koenig shoved his comlock back in its clip. Down
below, Carter climbed the ramp, swung himself up
the superstructure and heaved himself to the top
rib where he stood looking round the set. There was
still a good half hour of sweat and aching effort
before the Alphans could leave the road and make
the last sliding scramble to stand on the landing strip
and know they were home and dry.

Carter came to meet them and only then realised
the state they were in. Concerned, he began, "Commander . . ." and stopped with his hand going to his
head. It was the familiar pounding signal bringing ver-
tigo and he was half a minute bringing it under control
with the rheostat setting.

Already stupid with fatigue, the others were clumsy
and took longer. When Koenig cleared his eyes of double vision, he believed that Bergman's degaussers had
met their Waterloo and he was still out of sync with
the real world.

The set had filled up as though a chorus of seminude villagers had nipped smartly in from the wings. It had been a silent, barefoot rush from the edge of the vegetation and there was no doubt that the new arrivals had been playing a waiting game. Either they knew the effect was due and had been waiting for it, or they had fixed it as soon as the Alphans reached the clearing.

Helena, quicker off the mark with interpretation, said, "Copreons! Just like the picture."

There were some differences. The mob that had surged between the Alphans and Eagle Nine were small in stature, well made and athletico-somatic. Mainly men with a scattering of women. Dark haired, grey-green eyes, dressed alike in pleated green kilts of a kind of metal cloth. Every last one had a broad metal band round the temples. They looked tougher and more determined than their ancestors. Fighting for survival had sloughed off some of the fat.

Alan Carter knew for a truth he should have stayed in the Eagle until the stragglers were home. Laser in hand, he was prepared to cut himself a path. But Koenig forestalled him. "Hold it, Alan!"

The Copreons had arrived on silent feet and were still silent and stock still. It was like a passive-resistance demo. Nearest to the Alphans, a man and a woman stepped forward together, palms open and stretched out in the universal mime of peace and good will.

Koenig made a mental effort that came near to spraining his brain and shrugged off his fatigue.

Meeting like with like, he shoved his laser into its clip and went forward with open hands. Trying to pitch his voice right for friendly welcome he said, "Koenig. Commander Koenig. We are from Moonbase Alpha. Greetings."

It got close attention. The woman ran the tip of her tongue round her lips and looked at him with wide eyes.

He tried again. "We are from the Moon which has

appeared in your sky. We came to find out why the
people of this planet attacked our base without warning."

Surprisingly, there was an answer. Haltingly, using
a language which had been learned in a crash course,
the woman said, "We know. We have listened. Our
. . . com . . . puter . . . has analysed your speech."
She touched the firm point of her breast with a slim
finger, unconsciously falling into the pose of much re-
ligious art, and said, "I . . . am . . . Rama. This is
. . . Menos."

Menos was looking hard at Sandra Benes. She was
not a data analyst for nothing and moved half a step
nearer Paul. These Copreons might well have fallen
on austere times, but there was something in his eye
which seemed to be weighing her up as orgy potential.

Koenig said, "Since you have listened to us, you will
know why we are here. Perhaps you can explain why
we were attacked?"

Menos looked round the group of Alphans. Once
committed to speech he proved a better linguist than
Rama. "We know, Commander Koenig. Your Moonbase Alpha is a life raft that you maintain only by
constant effort. We can sympathise with you. Our case
is much the same. Except that, in this valley, we live
freely under the sun. But we are marooned here, as
surely as you are marooned on your dead asteroid.
You need rest and food. Come, we will show you how
we live and discuss our problems. It is possible that
we can help each other."

Victor Bergman said, "We have a time limit. The
moon will drift out of your gravisphere. We have to
return to our people."

Menos touched the metal band on his forehead.
"You know the magnetic effects here. I see you have
taken steps to protect yourselves. There is a wide fluc-
tuation and a period of maximum disturbance is very
near. It will be stronger than anything you have met
so far and your machine would be impossible to navigate. We have lived with these effects for a long time

and know how to deal with them. Our living quarters are screened. We can talk there."

Bergman looked at Koenig. Scientific curiosity never sleeps for long. He was clearly interested. For Koenig it was another matter. However peaceful the demonstration, the Copreons had prevented them from reaching Eagle Nine. That was a fact. If he had been fresh and full of natural aggro, he might have stuck with that and gone for a trial of strength. But to his jaded mind, the spiel had the ring of truth and reason. He nodded and Victor Bergman, for one, looked pleased and said, "Very well."

Rama and Menos looked at each other and both smiled. It could be that they were social types and liked to entertain the passing stranger, but a small alarm bell sounded in Koenig's head. Why should they care either way? What advantage were they looking for?

The agreement was well received by the main body. Some had been looking about uneasily as though the magnetic flux was likely to appear in physical form. Menos turned to them and spoke two words that fell on the ear like Arabic and there was a general move.

Seen close, the vegetation was higher than they expected. Feathery-topped grasses were shoulder high. Trees with broad spade leaves towered overhead. Beyond the first screen there was a path wide enough for four abreast and the crowd surged along it. There was no obvious discipline and yet no confusion.

There was not far to go. The path took a down turn and led between two walls of rock which had been machine cut. Fifty metres on, there was a square opening with a monolithic lintel. Inside, it was pink as a throat with fluted cladding to hide the rock and lights set in ceiling ports.

On the last stretch, Koenig had been conscious of pressures in his head and was ready to believe that Menos had been right about the force field. Inside the gallery, there was an instant change; confusion lifted. They had a screening system all buttoned up.

But a subdued thump from the rear had him spinning round on his heel. Doubt crowded in. The end of the tunnel had sealed itself from roof to floor with a solid shutter of the same pink hue as the rest of the decor.

He stopped dead and faced Menos. "Why have you done that?"

"Do not be concerned, Commander. It is just as easily opened. It completes the screening for all our comfort. Also, we have enemies."

"The androids?"

"Just so. It is a long time since they last tried to take us by surprise. But who can tell? It is better to be on guard. At these times when the magnetic flux is at greatest intensity, they have most power and illusions of grandeur. It is a bitter thing that those creatures should be in the air and we should be forced underground like rodents."

Rodents they might be, but the underground sanctuary had been set up with sophisticated care for creature comfort. The entry shaft ended in a huge regular hemisphere which was decorated like a baroque folly.

There was enough food for vision to bring the Alphans to a stop as they tried to organise the scene into understandable features. Halfway up the dome there was a continuous gallery with a richly carved balustrade. It was reached by three curving stairways set like the blades of a turbine and floating down to a clear circular area like a dance floor in the centre of the rotunda.

In a notional sense, the stairways divided the space into three sectors and the division was carried on by specialist use of the floor area. They were entering the leisure and recreation zone. Small white tables were dotted about, pot plants, couches, soft furnishings, alcoves, a free-standing screen showing a moving picture and piped music plaintive as a zither.

Over to the right, beyond the first stairway, was a dining area with a huge table in curved sections set in a ring formation round a fountain. Water jetted from

a nymph's navel and fell into a moon-shaped dish on
an eccentric cam. As it filled, it tipped and shot a bright
cascade into smaller vessels, which in turn shot their
load down the line.

The third sector had claimed Bergman's interest.
Its centrepiece was a perpetual-motion gimmick of
three huge bronze disks, high on a pedestal and cir-
cling endlessly on each other's rims. At ground level,
the walls were lined with hardware: computer panels
winking with coloured telltales, monitor screens, operating consoles. There were free-standing desks and
a duty force at work, bare to the waist, as were all the
Copreons, and looking out of place surrounded by
the trappings of high-level technology. Inside the hive,
headbands were not worn and, clearly, not needed.

It gave the lie to Meno's apparently spontaneous
gesture. The Copreons had not turned out to a man to
welcome the stranger. Behind the smiles and the open
palms, they were hardheaded realists and there had
been no break in essential services.

Menos gave them a minute to let the scene make its
impact. Better than any words, it showed that, marooned or not, the locals had a great deal going for
them. The Alphans would understand that they were
dealing with equals or, as he believed, superiors.

It was a lot to take in after a busy day. Koenig
sensed that Menos was waiting for some comment. A
guest has his duties. He said, slowly, "This is very impressive. Your race has climbed a long way up evolution's ladder. You could survive here indefinitely."

He missed Rama's quick look, but it was not lost on
Helena Russell. She had a question. Medical practice
has much to do with the very young and the very old.
She had seen neither. "All your people are in the prime
of life. Is there no ageing on Pelorus?"

Rama said, "For many centuries now, we Copreons
have known how to arrest the ageing process."

Alan Carter said, "It's the national costume keeps
libido at a surge. It's a life style we could introduce on
Alpha." He was looking at Rama with open admiration

and, although his meaning was a mystery to her, the vibrations were crystal clear. With an effort, she kept to the intellectual bit. "Our life span is not materially different from yours. But to the end of it, we are able to retain all our physical and mental powers."

Helena Russell tried the other end of the spectrum. "Children? Are there children in this community?"

A shadow crossed Rama's expressive face. "There are no children." She gave no further explanation.

"Then in a limited time the community must die out."

"Just so."

Menos was looking anxious, as though the conversation had taken an unwelcome turn. "Come. You must refresh yourselves. Then we will all join together for a banquet to celebrate this strange meeting of two peoples adrift in space." He clapped his hands. Half a dozen of the nearest Copreon women detached themselves from the crowd and approached with smiles and open hands, miming for the Alphans to follow them. They led to the nearest stairway and at the foot of the stairs each took a guest by the hand. There was one spare and, reacting sensitively to atmosphere, she lined up on Carter's free side.

It was a silent sequence, as though they were attended by deaf mutes. But the service was deft and gentle and courtesy could go no further. At intervals, arches led from the gallery into a honeycomb maze of inner passages and rooms. Decor was plushy and subtly stirring to the senses. First call was a trip through a series of baths from warm, relaxing foam to an astringent deluge of cool, scented sprays with intermediate stops on massage tables.

The attendants had stepped nimbly out of their kilts at first base and clearly worked on the thesis that the human frame was well known to one and all and had nothing surprising to offer in a purely therapeutic situation. In the dreamlike sequence it was an easy lead to follow, but at the end of the line, there was consumer resistance, when trim kilts were laid out for

public wear. Helena and Sandra settled for their simple inner suits and clipped on their service belts with
lasers and comlocks in their clips. Uniforms had been
cleaned and pressed. The three men shrugged into
full gear.

Still working in mime, the Copreons led the way to
a suite of rooms opening off a lounge area. Carter's
friends seemed unwilling to leave him, but finally
backed off with a last tug at the set of his jacket and
gestures that made it plain he only needed to ask.

Moved by a kind of common impulse, the Alphans
pulled up chairs and sat round a table. It was like a
conference in the command office on Alpha and with
much the same personnel to attend it. Koenig flipped
a memo pad from a breast pocket, wrote briefly and
pushed it before his neighbour. Victor Bergman
nodded and passed it on. It said, "Keep it general.
Very likely bugged."

When he had it back in front of him, Koenig said,
"The day has ended better than it started. Give or take
some minor differences, these people are like ourselves
with the same expectations. They want to talk. Now we
have the best part of Alpha's executive council round
this table. Could we recommend to our people that
we ask for an agreement with the Copreons for joint
occupation here? Would there be a balance of advantage?"

Bergman took the hint. For a credible discussion
there had to be a hostile witness. He said, "That's going too fast for me, John. We hardly know a thing about
them. Point one: As far as we know this may be the
only fertile plot on this planet. Would it support another three hundred people? Point two: Are we prepared to live indefinitely under a siege economy? It's
comfortable and it looks viable, but the androids have
the high ground. Do we want to start with a war on
our hands? Point three: There's no turning back. Once
we operate the Exodus plan, it's good-bye to Alpha. Is
this the planetfall we were looking for?"

"Sandra?" Koenig looked at his data analyst. There

was not a lot of hard fact to process, but her clear, precise voice made it sound official. "It is unlikely, Commander, that this is the only habitable place. Conditions which produced this valley will be repeated elsewhere. With the help and good will of the Copreons we could set up a community of our own. But we would live under constant strain from the magnetic forces. It is certainly not what we hoped for. But then, the statistical probability that we shall ever find our ideal home is so small . . . that, indeed, only a miracle could help us."

"Paul?"

"I agree with Sandra. It is far from ideal, but it could be the best we can get. I think it should be put to a full meeting of all sections for a decision."

"By the rule book, the final decision has to be mine; but I concede that the known opinion of all Alphans would have a big influence on it. What about you, Alan?"

"I've been a military pilot most of my working life. I guess I'm used to carrying out orders. I know my section. They'd be prepared to work something out here and go for a hot war against the androids. I leave it to professionals in other fields to sweat out the moral arguments. What I've seen I like."

Sandra widened her expressive eyes and he added courteously, "None can compare with our own companions, but they do have an agreeable knack."

Koenig had left Helena to the last. She had been sitting, chin on hand, blonde hair hanging forward and hiding her face. She lifted her head. "As I see it, there's a simple criterion. We want the life style we know. We want families and children and room for expansion and a natural life. We'll face hardship. We'll have to. But we want the possibility of a settled future. Can anybody say, honestly, he can see that on Pelorus?"

There had been no sound of approaching footsteps, but Rama was already well through the hatch. She had changed her kilt for a diaphanous red one and a large hexagonal jewel, hung on a gold chain, lay between her breasts. Palms out and smiling, she said, "The banquet is prepared. We wait for our honoured guests."

A man may smile and smile and be a villain. Koenig had a flash of intuition that the same could be true of even such a woman.

CHAPTER SIX

Marooned on Pelorus, they might be; but scratching a living from the bare rock, they certainly were not. The opulent banquet spread in the diner was luxury run amok. If there were no pearls dissolved in the goblets of green wine, it was only because the cook had not heard of it.

Koenig had the seat of honour on the top table with Rama on his left and Menos on his right. Dishes came in endless succession from serving hatches which had opened in the cyclorama and gave glimpses of a gleaming kitchen area. The nymph on the fountain filled her buckets with a soft plash, digestive music filtered from the very stone, lighting flushed and changed through every hue of the spectrum. It was a sustained battery on the senses; a public-relations exercise to end all.

Either the word had gone out that the Alphans were to be given the full treatment or the Copreons were natural hosts. There was a language barrier for the *hoi polloi*, but the two nudes smothering Alan Carter with welcome were managing to get their meaning across. Sandra Benes, though no prude, came close to hacking at her right-hand neighbour with an electrum carver.

In spite of all, Koenig had a feeling that the Copreons were holding back. They were keeping the wake within bounds that the Alphans would not find it too disturbing. For his own reasons, Menos wanted the alliance. But what could the Alphans bring to a community that had all it needed? They would be extra mouths to feed and would bring inevitable strains to such an enclosed society. Every effort he made to get a serious conversation under way was turned aside. After two hours, he was no nearer on hard information.

Menos clapped his hands and the assembly came to order. Eyes looking to the high table were brilliant and challenging. They would obey, but nobody was pretending to like it. He spoke slowly and clearly for a good minute. Reluctantly, the Copreons pushed away from the tables. The party was over. Good manners still had a toehold. Each bowed to the guests and gave the palms up gesture of good will. Then, in groups, they began to move away, some to the lounge area, some up the long stairways.

Menos said, "Your sleeping rooms have been prepared for you. It has been a tiring day. Feel free to withdraw whenever you wish."

Koenig said, "Your hospitality has been very generous. We have to thank you. But there must be discussions between us. You understand the time problem. We must talk."

Rama and Menos exchanged glances. Menos came to a decision and said shortly, "This way."

They all moved into the third sector, past the duty team of Copreons, who had remained on station through the social evening, and into a circular conference room, plain and functional, with chairs set round an oblong table and a panel of switchgear set at every place.

Menos said, "This is the meeting room for the council. On matters of great importance, we take corporate decisions, as you do."

It was a small slip, but Koenig knew for a truth that their discussion upstairs had been monitored, word for word. He said evenly, "That is the only way. Every man must feel that his opinions have been considered. In our system, we talk a matter out. The decision, when it comes, can never please all, but we aim to satisfy the majority and the others loyally abide by that."

"So it is with us."

"You have not said whether there are other valleys like this one."

"You have not asked."

"I am asking now."

Rama, anxious to avoid any appearance of secrecy, came in quickly, "You must understand. For centuries Copreon has used Pelorus as a quarry for a metal which does not exist on our own planet. We call it infrangom. It is light and very strong and does not corrode in the atmosphere. It is very important to us. A community was established here. Pelorus is a barren desert. This valley was engineered by our specialists to reproduce a piece of homeland on Pelorus. There is no doubt that other sites could be developed like this."

Victor Bergman said, "With immense outlay of power and labour. When this was done, there was the backup organisation of a whole planet. Are there local resources to do it again?"

Menos said, "With your help and technical skills, I see no reason why it should not be done."

Helena Russell asked a key one. "What happened to Copreon? Why did they abandon you? Surely they could send reinforcements to bring the androids under control?"

"There is no certain answer. We keep constant listening watch for news of the home planet. It is a long story, but, briefly, there was significant change in the magnetic fields around Pelorus. One theory is that the long mining operations finally altered the run of infrangom in this great chain of mountains. Also, the endless labyrinth of galleries and tunnels, with their mineral tracks and power circuits, are like the nerve structure of a brain. The androids understood that. They can draw energy from it. Conditions were such that the supply shuttles could not navigate. We were the last party of replacements. Some superior-grade androids became independent of computer control. They successfully concealed this fact and slowly worked to bring the whole android force under their own direction. We were forced to retreat to this area of old workings. Now, there is a kind of balance. They are not strong enough to mount a full-scale offensive against us. We could not defeat them without crippling losses."

Rama said bitterly, "But they know that time is on their side. We can not replace ourselves and will finally die."

The question had not been answered and Bergman put it again, "And Copreon?"

Menos said, "We do not know with any certainty. There was political unrest. Powerful interests opposed to each other. Perhaps there was war. The space programme was expensive and used up resources. The wealth from infrangom created envy. It could be that the space installations were a primary target for malcontents."

It figured. Koenig could envisage a similar situation arising for Alpha, if the moon had stayed in orbit round Earth planet. It was not impossible that a hot war down below might have effectively broken the complex communication service.

Helena Russell returned to another question which had been niggling in the back of her mind. "Have you voluntarily decided that there should be no children?"

Rama could not avoid a quick look at Menos. His face was impassive. She answered for both, "Our race is very ancient and has been at a high level of civilisation for many millennia. Fertility levels are low. But, in any event, sterilising procedures were carried out on all women before leaving Copreon for service on Pelorus. On return, after a five-year term here, the procedures were reversed. That is acceptable. But we do not have the medical knowledge or facilities to carry out such operations."

"But you have medical staff?"

"They are trained for diagnostic work, but the backup service was so regular, that any seriously ill patient was lifted out for treatment on Copreon. Our only qualified surgeon who might have carried out such operations was killed in an accident."

Sandra Benes, who had been looking through an observation port into the control room, said suddenly, "Commander!"

All eyes turned her way and she said in a rush, "I was thinking, Commander, that the equipment here is much more powerful than anything on Eagle Nine. Could we use it to try to raise Main Mission and put them in the picture?"

Koenig was sure that it was not what she intended to say, but the same question had been on his list. He looked at Menos for his reaction.

The Copreon was ready enough. "We can try, of course. Your moon is nearer than our planet. Just now conditions are at their worst. In the morning perhaps?"

Koenig stood up. "You have been frank and open with us. I will be equally frank with you. The decision to leave Moonbase Alpha and throw in our lot with you will not be an easy one. But it will be put fairly to our people. Tomorrow morning at first light we will prepare to lift off."

Menos made no comment. It was as good an exit line as another to close the long day's march.

Up aloft, covers had been rolled aside in three sleeping chambers. Beds were on the lines of well upholstered play pens and Koenig could have kept his party together in any one. But he went for a sober division by sex and seniority. He said, "Helena, you and Sandra in here, in the middle. Alan and Paul on your left. Victor and I will take this end one."

Sandra was trying to catch his eye and finally followed him into his room, coming close and touching the zip of his tunic. But it was not Eros biting her neck; it was communication. He took out his memo pad and she wrote in a rounded, feminine hand, "They were lying. They *can* reach Alpha. I saw a corner of a picture on their scanner. I'm sure it was Main Mission."

He nodded and passed the book over to Bergman. "Thank you, Sandra."

"Good night, Commander. Good night, Professor."

They both watched her trim action as she moved out. Bergman looked surprised. He turned the leaf over and wrote, "What are they playing at, then?"

Koenig shrugged. Aloud, he said, "Tomorrow is another day. I guess I've never been more ready to hit the sack. Good night, Victor."

"Good night."

There was no sound from outside the suite. Acoustic screening was first-class. They could have been with Cheops in his burial chamber. Koenig programmed himself to wake in a couple of hours and closed his eyes.

When he opened them and looked at his time disc, he was only half an hour over his self-imposed limit. He climbed carefully out of the play pen, slipped on his pants and foam-soled boots, buckled on his belt and stepped silently for the archway. Courtesy lights in the lounge area gave a dim glow, not enough to see into the middle room as he passed. But he could imagine Helena's sleeping face, lashes in even arcs, hair in a honey-blonde fan. Instead of all the endless march and countermarch, he ought to be in there, feeling the long, smooth run of her thigh, her head on his arm. Would it ever come? They were as far from a true landfall as they had ever been. He shut his mind to it and went on through the third arch, stopping inside to let his eyes adjust to the low lumen count.

Alan Carter was nearest the door, sleeping like a deckhand in the piping days of sail, ready to turn out when the main split. His laser was on a wristband and Morrow, two metres off across the diagonal, had every chance of getting a hole in his head, if a dream took a bad turn.

Koenig put pressure on his shoulder and packed all

the persuasion he could get into a whisper. "Alan. Steady as you go. It's Koenig."

There was a dicey, split second when Carter's finger's closed on the butt of his laser and it came round in a rush, looking for a target. Then he was saying "Commander?"

"Quietly. I want to take a look downstairs."

The lounge area was closed from the gallery by a hatch. There was no need for words, they knew each other too well. Koenig silently shifted the switchgear and Carter was flat back against the wall, out of sight as the door opened.

Koenig stepped through empty-handed, a man putting the cat out and taking a turn round the shrubbery. The first armed Copreon they had seen, with a bulbous blaster held two-handed, was standing with his back to the balustrade watching the opening. His mouth was opening for a warning shout and the gun was coming up to aim for Koenig's sternum, when Carter picked him off with a stun beam that hit with mathematical accuracy between his eyes.

They left him standing, rigid as a tin man. Light levels were low and the floor of the huge rotunda was in semidarkness. Shaded spot lamps threw bright patches like coins in a muddy pool. There was no movement on the gallery. The sentry was the only one. The main force was off stage, recharging its psychic batteries.

The Alphans circled the gallery and chose the stairway that took them farthest from the control area. There was no challenge as they went down and reached the cover of the lounge with its free-standing book racks and room dividers. At the nearest point they could get to the duty room, Koenig called a halt. There were two Copreons, a man and a woman, still serving the hardware.

It was not the time of day to be one hundred per cent vigilant and, in any event, they must have believed that the Alphans were no threat. The girl was sitting on the edge of a desk swinging her legs and drinking from a beaker. Her co-worker was running a finger down the hollow of her back. It was a clear case of making the best of the situation they were in.

Carter looked at Koenig and got a nod. There was all the time in the world to take aim. He sent a wide-angled stun beam across the floor and the action congealed with a leg in mid swing and a finger poised on the middle lumbar vertebra.

Koenig did a rapid tour of the consoles. Some monitors were set to watch the outer approaches to the valley. He recognised the opening of the pass and knew that they had been watched every step of the way. There was the darkened Eagle waiting on its pad. Two screens showed sections of underground tunnel, closed at the ends by massive hatches with wheel release gear. One showed a silent and empty monorail platform. It was the updated version of having scouts out round the hideaway. It had also come to suffer from the weakness of all defensive works: its flank could be turned by an enemy already inside the gate.

Some screens were blank. Koenig passed them; he was looking for something else. Victor Bergman or Sandra might have found it sooner, but he went to work methodically and finally isolated the operating console for the main scanner. Carter roamed about the perimeter keeping an all-round watch.

The switchgear was unfamiliar, but the years of piloting strange ships and using communications systems paid off. Koenig cleared his mind of every other thing and stared at the instrument spread until the working detail made a pattern.

When he finally moved and shoved down a banana key, the big screen glowed at the centre with a bright dot that expanded to fill the frame. It was the night sky of Pelorus. Stars like jewels on a black velvet pad. Tuned dead centre and mellowed by an apricot tint, Earth's ravaged moon was set up as the principal feature and must have been plotted to a centimetre and locked in vision by a constant tracking probe.

Apart from the occasional flicker as interference

beat the dampers, the picture was rock steady. Koenig
selected another stud and was on familiar ground.
Main Mission had a full operations staff. He seemed to
be looking down at his command island from a point
high on the communications post. David Kano, at the
command desk, looked as though he had not left it
since Eagle Nine blasted off and had no intention of
moving. Tanya was clearly worried about him and appeared at his side with a tray of coffee and sandwiches.
Kano was calling slowly and deliberately on the Eagle
command net and although he was no lip reader, Koenig could get the message: "Alpha to Eagle Nine. Do
you read me? Come in Eagle Nine."

With the gear they had, the Copreons could have
been beamed into Alpha for days or weeks before
their planet was ever picked out of the cosmic ragbag
by Sandra's skillful hand. Koenig had to work with
trial and error for a couple of minutes before Kano's
voice was backing up the picture and Carter was
across at a spring. "You got through to Alpha,
Commander?"

"One way."

"Can you speak to them?"

It took longer and Carter was looking at the lay
figures at the desk and debating how long it would be
before they were taking up where they left off. Then
Koenig had the method and Main-Mission staff were
looking incredulously at the big screen.

Koenig said urgently, "Commander to Alpha. We
are down on Pelorus. Expect another communications
blackout. We aim to leave by first light in Eagle Nine.
Navigation round Pelorus hazardous. Magnetic fields.
Pinpoint this signal as a reference. Do you read me?"

Kano was equally quick, packing it in without
asking questions, "I read you, Commander. Do not
delay liftoff. Calculations now show an increase in
velocity. Moon contact with Pelorus will be shorter
than we thought. Do you want backup support?"

"How much shorter?"

"There are variables. Estimate only, three days

shorter. You must leave within eighteen hours for optimum window. I repeat, do you want backup?"

"On that time scale, one Eagle hazarded is one too many. We'll make it. There's another time scale running out right now. Over and out."

They heard Kano say, "Good luck, Commander." and Koenig was flipping switches to restore status quo.

In Main Mission, there was a buzz of conversation to break the hush and Kano had to quell it for a little service. He said, "Tanya, Leanne, I want that sequence rerun frame by frame. See what you can pick up. There's a limited view of the pad they're in. One thing's sure, it's not Eagle Nine. Alan's waving a laser. Piece it together and see what we have."

Alan Carter was looking at his living tableau. He took the beaker from the girl's hand and set it on the desk. The moving finger was developing a twitch and was ready to move on. He said "The effect's wearing, Commander. We don't have too much time."

As a last check, Koenig punched along the row of dark screens. He saw Bergman lying on his back, mouth open, very human and vulnerable for a man of science. Morrow was dead to the world. Still searching, he brought up an empty bed and one that was over full, where some of the home team were still batting. Carter began, "Commander . . ." and Koenig left it.

They went up the long stair at a run and were through the hatch into the lounge area as the guard completed his move and raised his gun to aim at the blank panel. He had not seen Carter and the image, still flickering on his retina, was the tall figure of the leading Alphan, standing in the opening and making no threatening move. He brushed a hand across his eyes. Vision playing tricks? He had no wish to look a fool. He stepped across to the door and examined it, undecided.

Down below, the duo were back on circuit with the girl looking at her empty hand and saying in sultry

Copreon, "You do have an eloquent forefinger, Orcus. I've gone all goosey and I don't recall putting that glass there. Just look at me."

Orcus swivelled her round to do that thing. It was true. He said, "Relief's due in thirty minutes. Be patient, my flower. Get your can off of my table top and take a walk round the shop. Meanwhile, I'll get that duty report drafted."

Up aloft, the guard had come to a decision. Taking it real slow and making no noise, he rolled the hatch. The lounge area was empty. He stepped quietly across to the right-hand arch and looked inside. There was enough light for him to make out two figures lying on the bed. He missed out the middle room and looked in the left-hand one. Two more. Silently, he went back the way he had come. It was all a black mystery, but the count was right. He began to walk up and down in front of the door. He knew Menos. If he was found asleep at his post, it would be a flogging and ten days solitary at the least count. He reckoned soberly, he had been saved by the bell.

Unseen inside the burrow the spectacular, apricot dawn of Pelorus was filling the valley with the outriders of a new day, when Koenig rolled out and brought his scientific adviser back on stream.

Victor Bergman sat up and ran his fingers over his thinning hair. The rest had sharpened up his computer and he had a whole raft of questions that needed answers. But he recognised that it was not the time. One calculation, which had been running through his unconscious mind while it was off load, had implications which perhaps the Copreons already knew. There would be no harm in their hearing it. He said, "You remember when we first worked out a likely trajectory for the moon's passage through this gravisphere?"

"We feared there might be devastation on Pelorus

and damage to centres of population. Now we see
there's nothing to fear from that."

"That's partly right. These bunkers should be
secure enough. But there will be effects."

"Such as?"

"The moon's mass is big enough to distort these
magnetic fields. It could affect the androids and our
first estimates of passage could be way out. Action
and reaction. The moon won't get clear scot free."

"The screens will protect Alpha."

"Correction, John. We *hope* the screens will protect Alpha. We should raise Main Mission as soon
as we can and get Kano working on it."

Paul Morrow was in through the arch and looking
around, clearly a puzzled man. He said, "They're not
with you then?" and Koenig saw the row of monitors
down below and the snap picture of the empty bed.

"Helena and Sandra?"

"The same."

Koenig brushed past him, striding through into
the middle room and on into the washroom. It was
empty. Except for a faint trace of sandalwood in the
still air, there was nothing to show that the Alphan
women had ever been on the set.

Outside, the hive was stirring. Some Copreons were
on the gallery, others had already gone down and were
dotted about the floor of the rotunda.

Koenig picked the nearest, shoved a hand flat on
his chest and backed him to the balustrade. Hawk
face grim, he said, with a cold menace that needed no
translation, "Menos. Where is Menos?"

There was no doubt that the man understood. The
danger he was in of taking a dive over the rail sharpened his mind. Taking care to make clear that he,
personally, was a man of peace, he mimed that he
would be glad to act as a guide.

There was not far to go. Menos, with Rama by
his side, appeared on the gallery from his own suite
of rooms, spruce and fresh for the day's march in
a well-pressed kilt. No armed Copreons were about,

but instinct told Koenig there must be some close at hand. Menos looked too complacent, as though he knew that he had the cards stacked in his favour.

He had to be admired in one sense. He was trading his own life on the speed of someone else's reaction times. Koenig stopped two metres off. Alan Carter sidestepped to the gallery wall and put his back to it. If there was anything fancy going on, he was placed to see all angles.

The move was not lost on Menos, but his smile of welcome never faltered. "Good day to you, Commander. You will eat with us? Then we will escort you to your spacecraft."

"Where are they, Menos?"

"I do not have the pleasure of understanding you, Commander."

"You understand well enough. Where are our companions, the two Alphan women?"

"Are they not in their room?"

Paul Morrow broke in angrily, "You know damn well they're not."

Menos ignored him and kept his eyes fixed on Koenig. "They can not be far away, Commander. Women have a natural curiosity. It is likely that they were up before you and decided to look around. I will make enquiries. The duty staff may have seen them. We will go downstairs. Come with me."

In the lounge area, there was some negative evidence. Four of Bergman's degaussing helmets were on a table where they had been placed the night before. Two were gone. Menos said nothing and let the discovery speak for itself. He gathered a crowd of Copreons and spoke rapidly in gobbledygook. Actors to a man, the Copreons looked all astonishment and one girl answered with frank, open gestures as though she were all agog to help the fuzz with their enquiries.

Menos said, "It is as I thought. Cilla believes she saw them. She was one of the first to come down. She says they took their helmets and walked out towards the entrance. She assumed they intended to look at the valley or perhaps to walk as far as your ship."

"Through the sealed hatch?"

"There would be no problem in that, Commander. The opening mechanism is very easy to understand and your charming and intelligent friends would have no difficulty in finding the correct procedure."

"Suppose we go and take a look and suppose you come with us in case anybody gets any foolish ideas?"

"I am not sure that I follow you, Commander; but, of course, I will accompany you on your search."

Koenig said with cold sincerity, "Let me make it very clear. If anything has happened to them and the fault is at your door, a great many Copreons will end up dead."

Neither Rama nor Menos reacted. Their smiles might have been the same if he had been promising a gold brick to each and every one. In its way, it was as effective as a bland, Oriental mask to conceal true feeling. Or, maybe, they believed they had it so well organised that there was nothing to fear.

They had gone ten paces when Koenig saw that every Copreon in view was wearing a headband. He said, "Alan, the helmets." and Carter strode back to pick them up.

Menos said, "A wise precaution, Commander. The severe phase has passed, but there is always a residual flux which has to be guarded against."

"Now you tell me."

"I was concerned about the search for your companions."

Outside, it was cool and pleasant, hardly more than twenty Celsius. There was a damp smell and small droplets of water glistened on the fern fronds and the leaves of the cycads. Menos said, "There is no natural rain on Pelorus. Every night, a sprinkler system operates for three hours. Without it, this valley would become a desert."

Morrow said, "On our proving orbit we saw evidence of other vegetation, large-scale forestation, for instance."

Rama answered too quickly. In spite of the surface unconcern, the action was working on her judgement and she gave something away. "Your experience should tell you that all is not as it seems on Pelorus. The lichen would appear to be a natural grass, but your ship would have been destroyed by it. Only infrangom, of the metals we know, can stand against it. Vegetation here is not on a straight biological pattern. There is an electrochemical complication."

It registered in Koenig's head. There had not been a minute since their arrival in the gravisphere that had been free from the Copreon monitors. He was striding it out and the Copreons were having to work to keep their smiles fixed and stay with him. As the party broke from cover into the clearing, he said curtly, "You would have saved us a journey, if you had answered our signals and told us that."

Menos said, "But, as I understand it, the androids made forceful demonstrations to keep you away and you ignored them. You are very determined people and like to see for yourselves. You would not have believed, until you had seen with your own eyes."

Morrow and Carter were up the slope at a run. They disappeared into Eagle Nine's open hatch. As the rest reached the pad, Morrow reappeared. "Not a sign, Commander. They're not here."

Koenig's laser was already out of its clip. He spoke to Menos and the brutal rasp he got into it carried enough conviction to put a check on the smiler. He was aiming at Rama's neat navel and had first pressure on the firing stud. "Don't push me, Menos. Where are they? I'll start with your friend. Being a considerate man, I'll count to five and you can say good-bye to her."

There was no doubt Menos felt the pressure. Without the smile, his face had a new look. If Helena

Russell had been there to observe it, she would have classified it feature by feature on the Piderit scale as a classic. Mouth was grade six, stubborn and unpleasant. Eyes fixed on Koenig's finger were grade four, attentive. Nose wrinkled to the root was miming unpleasant reflection. Brows were corrugated. A group of judges would have picked it out from a pile of photo-fit examples as belonging to a man who would have no chance to make friends and influence people.

Another element in it was bothering Koenig as he worked slowly through his countdown. There was no concern for Rama. The Copreon had been prepared to take a calculated risk. He was waiting for a pay-off.

There was no wavering in Koenig's eyes. There was no doubt that he would do what he said he would do. It convinced Victor Bergman, for one, and knowing his friend, he reckoned it was something he would have trouble to live with. As Koenig's cold voice counted, "Two," and Rama's hands clenched at her sides, he stepped forward. "John! You can't . . ."

It went unfinished. Menos had lifted his right hand shoulder high. Bergman felt a force hit the top of his balding head as though he had been struck by an unseen club. Darkness flooding in like a tide, he saw Koenig fighting to stay on his feet and the bright thread of a laser beam searing into the ground between himself and Rama.

CHAPTER SEVEN

Helena Russell swung her long legs out of the narrow bed she was in and looked around the set. She could have been anywhere in the galaxy where an advanced culture had reached the stage of setting up a medicentre with every refined technical aid at the physician's hand.

It was a four-bed ward, white and clinical, seemingly without doors or windows and lit by oval ceiling ports. The whole of the wall facing the beds was taken up by hardware, some of which she recognised as similar in design and function to the gear in her own sick bay on Moonbase Alpha.

First things first, she checked out herself. Slim as a spear, she stood on warm thermoplastic tiling and took a couple of steps. No problem. She was all systems go. There was a tall locker by the bed head, which opened at a touch. Inside was a white Copreon kilt and a pair of thonged sandals. The only item of her own kit was the Bergman patent degaussing helmet.

Two beds off, Sandra Benes was a pale ivory lay figure. Professionalism never sleeps. Helena went to her bedside and picked up a wrist to check pulse rate. It was steady and dead on normal. Following some subconscious logic of her own, Sandra said, "Paul . . ." then her eyes opened wide and data acquisition networks made corrections. "Doctor. Dr. Russell."

"It's all right. Another of their fancy drugs. If it goes on like this, we'll end up as addicts."

"We? Where are the others?"

"Not here for a sure thing. But, having said that, I wouldn't know where."

"They'll be looking for us."

"If they can."

Quietly spoken, it opened up a whole range of possibilities. Arms on her knees and chin on her arms, Sandra looked soberly at the equipment spread. It was all go. This was one more twist of a convoluted screw. As if they did not have enough problems, keeping Alpha's life-support systems at the bubble. When, if ever, would they come across a simple and uncomplicated race of people, who would be sincere and open and give them an honest welcome? Every new attempt they made seemed doomed from the start. Everybody had problems of their own or wanted to impose some alien pattern on the Alphans.

Aloud she said, "I suppose it's the same on Earth planet, when you think of it."

Not having all the argument, Helena was lost. "What is?"

"Factions. Power groups wanting to push their own programmes. Somebody gets an idea and, who knows, it might be a good idea in itself; but first crack out of the bag and they get *fanatical* about it. With the best motives, they use brute force to get their message home."

"Any means justified, if the end's right."

"That's it. But it just isn't true. Means have a way of altering ends. History proves it, over and over again. Why can't these people be frank and tell us what they want? What do they expect from us?"

"It can only be something they believe we wouldn't accept given free choice."

"We should try to get out of here."

Helena Russell went to her locker, snapped on her kilt and put on the sandals. It was half way to feeling fully clothed and in her right mind. Sandra did the same. Starting at either end, they made a slow circuit of the walls. The white enamelled cladding was in sections. Any one panel could be a door. None moved a millimetre under any kind of pressure.

They were still working methodically, when a whole unit of oscilloscopes pivoted on its base and Rama was in through the gap followed by a couple of Copreon men and four women. As a gesture towards medical etiquette, all except Rama wore white kilts and the women had broad electrum armbands bearing pictographs of a syringe and a lotus plant. Helena Russell had walked into too many sick bays in similar company to be in any doubt. It was a medical team doing the rounds.

There was no surprise that the patients were up and about. Rama, less smiling than usual, said formally, "Good day, Dr. Russell."

Helena left the wall she was testing and walked to meet them. Her particular style of blonde beauty was a new thing to the Copreons and all eyes tracked her in. Keeping her voice steady and matter of fact, she said, "It will be a good day when we are in our ship and returning to base. Since you have listened so much to our speech you must know that our intentions were peaceful. Let us go as we came and very soon our moon will take us out of your system."

"I regret, that is not possible."

"Do you regret it or is that another meaningless phrase?"

"In a certain sense. Other things being equal, I would rather have people pleased with what they are doing than otherwise."

Sandra Benes said bitterly, "But if what pleases them doesn't happen to please you, something has to give and you prefer your own way."

"Just so. Every living organism engineers the environment, as far as it can, to give itself the maximum satisfaction."

Helena Russell had to concede that Rama had a powerful argument. Hedonist philosophy made a thick strand in human thinking. It was always a minority who could take the transcendental view and put themselves out of the centre slot. This time, they seemed to be getting Rama on a clear line. Maybe she would be prepared to say exactly what Copreon intentions were.

Helena said, "What you say is partly true and partly not true, the debate still goes on. Are you ready, yet, to be frank with us and tell us what you have in mind for us?"

Rama gave a curt gesture to her backup force. The two men went to work and wheeled out examination chairs, with headrests and footstalls set wide apart. The four nurses peeled off, two to each Alphan and waited for the next word.

Rama said, "You can make this uncomfortable for yourselves or easy. There is nothing, in fact, to fear. You are to be given a thorough medical examination. You, at least, Dr. Russell, will see nothing strange in that."

The chairs were ready, plugged to the keyboard of a diagnostic computer. The nurses moved in, taking an arm each. Helena Russell considered it. She could struggle or she could walk. The end would be the same. It was better to walk and keep some kind of dignity. She threw off the two helping hands and walked firmly to the nearer chair.

The Copreon operator, clearly very familiar with the technique, slipped two fingers in her waistband and whipped off her kilt. In three seconds flat she was staked out, ankles gripped by bands of infrangom, wrists strapped down to the armrests, head clamped to the stall.

Keeping her voice steady and professional, Helena said, "What is the purpose of this examination? Alphans have regular medichecks. We carry no diseases which would harm you."

Rama was looking thoughtfully at Helena. She had

seen the impact that was being made on the Copreon
men. By her own philosophy, she was all for
maximising on the pleasure principle; but suppose,
for instance, this spectacular blonde creature should
become the court favourite? It was an angle she
would have to watch. There was a little of the dark
pleasure of malice in her voice as she said, "I will
tell you what is intended for you, Dr. Russell. You
will remember that I said the Copreon women are
sterile and that the medical skills available here
could not help us. That was not strictly true. We have
a competent medical team; but we do not have supplies of a certain drug, which is the key element in
reversal procedures."

Helena said, "It is possible that our resources on
Alpha could help you."

"I think not. But there is something we can do.
First we have to assess your compatibility. You understand that transplant surgery has always had problems where host tissues and donor tissues do not
match. Rejection occurs. We must check this and
calculate what, if any, modification is needed for the
Alphan body to match our own."

Perhaps it would have been more reasonable to
struggle to the last step. Helena felt suddenly sick.
Sandra had been following the dialogue like a tennis
umpire and began to heave away at her retaining
straps, dark eyes brilliant with a mixture of anger
and simple fear. She fairly spat out, "Don't think
you'll get away with this. Alphans will avenge us.
You are signing a death warrant for your people."

"You have probably misunderstood me. No harm
is intended to you. You will simply carry out your
function as women. You will act as hosts to Copreon
foetuses. Fertilised eggs will be implanted in the
uterus. You will bear the child. Its biological parents
will be Copreon. The gestation period is shorter for
us. We calculate that each of you, with care and
attention, will bear two children each year. This will

give our people new hope while they work on their long-term project."

Helena said, "That could only be done with our co-operation and you will not have it."

"Don't deceive yourself, Doctor. One way or another, we will get it. Now, there are other matters I have to attend to. I leave you in attentive hands."

Sandra had stopped struggling. One of the nurses had picked up a hypo gun and was examining the charge setting. The Alphan said quickly, "All right. That won't be necessary."

The nurse looked across at Rama who had stopped at the hatch and got a curt nod. As a parting shot Rama said, "We are very reasonable. If you co-operate, you will be treated well. But if it becomes necessary, you will be kept under sedation."

The hatch closed at her back and the medical team went silently to work. Blood tests, smears, the whole range of data for their computer to go to work on. When it was done, the leading Copreon tore a long printout from the outfall and looked at it with every satisfaction. He spoke in Copreon and it was clear that it was all good news. They were in business.

A nurse asked a question and got a short answer which was clearly a negative. The team tidied the work area and gathered at the hatch. With a final look at the Alphans and a comment which raised a general laugh, the leader opened up and all went through. One minute the ward had seemed over full and very busy, the next it was quiet as a grave and empty except for the Alphans.

Sandra said, "Can they do it, Dr. Russell."

"There's nothing against it. The technique was developed on Earth planet a few decades ago. It was never much used. Our problem was to control fertility rather than increase it. It's an established practice for stock improvement, getting a good breeding animal to bear other strains more efficiently."

The chairs had been left at full tilt, so that the

Alphans were lying almost horizontal. As she spoke, Helena had been rocking herself backwards and forwards, throwing her weight as far as she could to press her heels against the footrests and then her shoulders against the flat leatherette back. She was getting two of three centimetres of free movement.

Sandra Benes saw the move and joined in enthusiastically on her own account. She also went on talking, recognising that there could well be a monitor on listening watch. "Rama said something about another project they have in the long term. What could she mean by that?"

"I've been thinking about it. Two things possibly. One would be getting control of the whole planet again. The other would be trying to leave altogether and get back to Copreon."

"They said there were no ships."

"What they say and what the truth is, can be different."

"There could be a building programme. They might have a damaged ship somewhere that they aim to repair."

"Copreon is likely to be out of range for Eagle Nine, but they could use parts of her in their own craft."

There was no reply from Sandra. She was a surprised girl. A last frenetic thrust had beaten the ratchet stop and her chair had slammed forward. As the footrests swung down for a full due and thumped into the pedestal supports, there was a definitive click and the ankle bands snapped open. At the same time, the headband swivelled away.

Without the wrist straps holding her arms, she would have been thrown flat on the parquet. As it was, she believed her shoulders would never be the same again as they took the strain.

But she was free to move. Squatting under the curve of the chair, with an ache in every joint, she got her teeth to the right-hand strap and worked at it, blood dropping on her heaving chest as the metal toggle cut into her mouth.

When her right hand came free she was sobbing with effort and had to clear sweat from her eyes. Then she was plucking the other strap away and dropped on all fours like a bemused hound dog. She crawled over to Helena and hauled herself to her feet using the chair as a prop. Swinging her weight with Helena's she threw the chair past its stop and came near to getting herself flattened.

When Helena was free, they stood for a minute out of programme. At any time the medical circus could be in again. It was obvious that they should move on and try to reach Eagle Nine. Grabbing up kilts, sandals and degaussing helmets, they looked at the hatch panel. They had seen it used twice as an exit and the release gear had to be somewhere on the panel of the oscilloscope spread. Sandra found it by a natural flair for identifying switchgear and, as she pushed over the lever, Helena rummaged along the counter for a hypo gun.

As the panel pivoted clear, a Copreon with a blaster on a shoulder strap, who had been standing with his back to it, spun round on his heel to see what was o'clock and Helena sent a full charge of a pinky grey serum into his bare chest. He was out like a light and they caught him as he fell, holding him upright, until Sandra had found the closing switch and the hatch was shut. They left him leaning on it, eyes wide open and a fixed smile on his ageless face.

In the clearing, close to Eagle Nine, Koenig was on his feet and telling himself that he was not fit to command a scout troop. Menos had outsmarted him all along the line. It was humiliating.

Paul Morrow joined him, then Carter. Victor Bergman was slower; but when he finally scrabbled to his feet, he was first with a theory. "That was a *selective* strike, John. No doubt about that. They had us monitored every step of the way. You saw Menos raise his hand? That was cool. He took a chance there. He finally realised you would do it."

Carter said, "But why be that elaborate? They could have taken us at any time. When we were asleep, for instance, as they took Dr. Russell and Sandra."

Koenig said, "We'll use the Eagle and blast through the door. This time, they won't have it so easy."

First off the mark, he was first to come to a grinding halt as he butted into a free-standing, transparent barrier that blocked his way. Ten minutes later he was convinced. Eagle Nine was sealed in a protective screen that put her out of reach. The Copreons had done it again. Coming back to Carter's question, he had to ask himself what all the gestural dance was about. It had to be that Menos had some purpose which he had not yet revealed. Maybe, in the short term, he was just a shrewd operator who was minimising casualties for his own side. In the long term, he had other plans.

Bergman was on the same frequency. As they met at the top of the slope, after a fruitless circle of the enclosed Eagle, he said, "Perhaps they want more Alphans down here. They must consider that the time is running out and our people will know that. Another party could be trapped. But why?"

Koenig was looking across the valley to the dark mouths of the old workings. He said, "The rotunda we were in was the admin centre for the mining projects in this area. The galleries over there could lead to off-shoots of the complex. If we can get back inside, we could find some answers."

Carter said, "What about the front door? They might not expect anybody to be so stupid as to try that."

"We'll try that first."

Heat was already moving up the scale as the sun jacked itself higher over the rocky rim of the valley. The trees gave shade, but also they gave cover. Each Alphan had an acute sense of being watched. To Koenig, it was no surprise when he was brought up short by a familiar force-field barrier set across the defile.

The Copreons had legislated even for fools, or they were monitoring every move and knew precisely where the Alphans were heading. Which it was, became clear as Koenig struck off left through the bush aiming for the valley side. After a hundred metres of rough travel through vegetation as dense as any rain forest, they hit another stop. The Copreons had dropped another shutter.

Koenig said, "How are they doing it, Victor?"

"Body heat, brain currents, you name it. We can do pretty well ourselves with life-sign monitors for crews on mission."

Morrow put his finger on a flaw. "Surely, we can, Professor; but all we know is whether the man is still alive. We can't say to a metre where he is."

"It wouldn't be too difficult, working a couple of co-ordinates."

"Not if he stayed still; but we're moving."

Bergman stuck doggedly to his theory. "It has to be something that we transmit like a homing beacon. Nothing visual would work in this country."

Koenig thumped the heel of his hand on his forehead. It was no time for academic discussion. He could imagine Helena Russell inside the hill and the nudge of a sixth sense was telling him that she was in trouble.

His hand hit the stud of his degaussing helmet and, like Archimedes in his bath, he could say he had it in a flash. He whipped the helmet off and handed it to Bergman. "What about this, Victor?"

Victor Bergman looked at it and, for once, was slow off the mark. "I don't follow you, John. There's nothing in that circuit that would act as a transmitter."

"Not the way you fixed it, but these helmets were out of our sight for too long. Anybody could have planted a self-energising beacon. We probably show up on a scanner as four silver stars."

Bergman checked Sandra's neat wiring. Nothing had been added or modified. He pulled the rubber grummet from its groove and checked round the rim.

When he had it, he held it out in the palm of his hand, moving it slowly, so that the distant operator would not suspect that it was no longer being worn. Koenig picked it off carefully and set it head high on the bole of a massive tree. It was a thick, dime-size circle with an adhesive back. Every helmet was carrying one and they set them in line facing the invisible screen.

Carter said, "They might reckon we could stumble on that with good luck and a following wind. Would there be any more?"

They had one more each. Carried under the instep of the left shoe in every case. Carter said, "They're a right lot of particular, farsighted bastards and that's a fact."

The Alphans retraced their steps for fifty metres, turned left, pushed on parallel to the entry ramp to the rotunda and then veered left again. There was no check. This time they were free to move on, until Koenig had one last screen of fronds between himself and open country. He raised a hand to halt the column.

The nearest opening in the rock face was set on a broad ledge that had once carried a mineral track and ran below the roadway they had walked down. It was twenty metres above the valley floor and, except for the top five metres which were sheer, it was an easy scramble.

Sooner or later, the monitoring team in the rotunda was certain to look at the stationary blips on the scanner and put two and two together. The less time taken now in hanging about, the better.

Koenig said, "One at a time. Once you're in the open, move it along. Up you go, Alan."

Carter crossed the narrow strip at a run. They watched him make the scramble look easy; then he had to traverse to find a viable route. Once he had it, he was away again. Koenig had been timing the operation. As Carter heaved himself onto the ledge, he said, "Two minutes on the nose. It's still a long time if there's anybody looking for a target. See what you can do, Paul."

Morrow had the advantage of seeing it done and knocked five seconds off.

Koenig said, "Victor. No records to break, but as fast as you like."

Although he seemed to be slow and deliberate, Victor Bergman was only fractionally over average time for the course. Koenig spent the time trying to make sense of the random scatter of old workings. Each one had its individual track. They had a long-abandoned look as though they had been used by early miners using simple techniques. But any community able to run space shuttles across a solar system would have been equipped from the start with highly sophisticated gear. Maybe there had been people on Pelorus even before the Copreons had made the trip?

It was a thought to share with the amateur archaeologist. Helena Russell appeared in his mind's eye and he told himself bitterly that his own lack of foresight had put her in Menos's hands. They should have jacked it in and turned for Alpha as soon as Eagle Nine was ready for flight. He saw Bergman reach journey's end and was off himself, in a controlled burst of effort which got him into the cave before the scientist had dusted himself off.

The shaft sloped gently down and two square section ruts a metre apart suggested that ore tubs had been run on some kind of wheeled system. But all gear had been stripped out. There was no rusting pick head or lamp sconce to show how the old miners had gone to work.

The other three had already made adjustments to their comlocks to get a pencil beam of visible light instead of the operating beam. Koenig said, "We don't know how long we shall have to search. One comlock at a time to conserve power. Let's go."

For three hundred metres it was straight and all down hill. Paul Morrow voiced the doubt that was in every head. "There's no saying that these old workings were ever brought into the system. God knows where this leads, but it's going the wrong way."

Carter said, "We could spend months checking out every shaft. For that matter, if they were all connected, there'd be no need to make new approach roads. They could have pulled all the ore out of one or two main routes."

Thin veins of infrangom showed up as Koenig's searching beam probed ahead. He reckoned they both had a point. But he also remembered the closed hatches he had seen on the Copreon scanner. There was a watch kept on entry from other tunnels. They had to come from somewhere and, by any reasoning, were likely to go through the hills and meet up with the androids' sector.

He set himself another ten minutes. After that, they would work back and pick another hole.

There was a half minute still to run and he was going on only because he had fixed a limit and any system was better than no system, when the beam hit a stop and splayed out in an asterisk of light. The tunnel was blind. It was a long folly going nowhere.

Seen close, it was clear that a section of roof had come down. The parallel ruts ran on to the face and were blocked by rubble. Alan Carter, out of simple frustration heaved away at a long slab and Koenig grabbed for his waist and shoved him bodily aside.

There was a sliding rumble as the filling settled to a new level and the spot where Carter had stood was thigh deep in broken rock. Dust had risen in a cloud and was wafted back up the tunnel by a draught of warm air.

Carter picked himself up. "Thanks, Commander. Sorry about that. I guess it could have brought the roof in."

"Don't apologise. You did well. Look at that."

The loose rock had rolled away from the right-hand wall and for the first time they were seeing evidence of a branch gallery. Up close to the roof, there was a metre-wide hole that a careful man might crawl through.

Taking it real slow, as if he were walking on eggs, Koenig went up the pile of scree and shoved head and shoulders through the gap. His voice filtered back. "This could be it. Watch how you go."

Journey's end, when they were all gathered at floor level, was an interchange point in the system. It was a hemisphere on a twenty-metre diagonal, with a turntable set in the rock, operated by a lever and a pawl-and-ratchet device. Ore cars could be switched and shunted off through a number of connecting tunnels. Only a set of mine drawings could make sense of the layout, but there was one tunnel that led back the way they had come. It was still sloping down hill.

Bergman said, "There's no doubt about it, John. We're well below the level of any outlet on the hillside. This is going below the valley floor. It's the right direction."

This time there were choices to be made. Fifty metres on there was an intersection and another turntable. Koenig stopped. He reckoned that they might have to come back in darkness. The turntable operating lever was a loose fit in its socket and he heaved it out, laying it in the centre of the roadway they had come down. Two minutes later, they were facing a three-way junction.

There was nothing to choose. Koenig tried to imagine how they were placed with relation to the ground above. "What do you think, Victor?"

"Not left, but nothing in it for centre or right. They must both go roughly for where we want to be."

"Centre then."

There was no loose stone about and he used his laser sparingly to mark the floor with a thin smear of instant lava. The slope was levelling off. They were meeting intersections every few minutes. Koenig checked his time disc. They had more than made up the time in the first tunnel; they must be under the valley floor.

Alan Carter whose hearing was uncanny, put a hand on Koenig's arm. "Commander!"

"What is it?"

"Do you hear anything?"

Paul Morrow said, "Like what, Alan?"

"A faint hum. Machinery of some kind."

Fifty paces on, it was clear to all hands. Bergman knelt down and put his ear to the roadway. "There's no doubt, John. It's machinery. There's a powerhouse somewhere. They must use a lot in that rotunda."

"But a mine shaft wouldn't open out from a power-house."

"I don't think these workings have anything to do with the Copreon organisation. They predate the present generation of Copreons. As I see it, they used this site because it was ready-made to build their working colony on; but their recent mining was highly mechanised with android labour and could be well away from here."

It was all interesting speculation, but Koenig was not in the mood. Streaked with sweat and dust and sick to his stomach with all things Copreon, he wanted out and if he could get out by walking on Menos, it would be all gain. He came as near as he had ever come to snapping at his old friend. "I'm sure you have the right of it, Victor. Put it in the log."

The vibration of the unseen generators reached a maximum and began to fade. Koenig turned on his heel and strode back along the tunnel to the intersection closest to the point of maximum noise. He said, "Paul and Victor, go along that way. Not far. I don't want us losing each other in this maze. Two minutes, then back here. Check out whether you get nearer."

With Carter, he took the opposite limb and it was clear in the first half minute, they had backed a loser. When they joined forces again, Paul Morrow was looking more cheerful than at any time since. "Progress, Commander. We're home and dry."

In a manner of speaking, he was right, but on any sober count there was a lot more mileage to go before they could do any congratulating.

Morrow's tunnel ran out into an enclosed quarry feature which was big enough to lose the beams of the comlocks in its lofty roof. It was on a similar scale to the Copreons' living rotunda and gave force to Bergman's theory that the Copreons had taken over existing works and adapted them to their own use. It even had a gallery hewn out of the rock, halfway up the dome. Instead of elaborate flying stairways, there were vertical ladders in pairs at intervals.

Unrepentant, Bergman was at it again. "What do you think about that, John? It's the most amazingly economical system I've seen. You see each ladder is free to move up and down one step. There's an eccentric cam. One lifts, one stays still. Anybody going up, gets on one ladder and it lifts him one rung. Then he swings over to the stationary ladder and the first one falls back. The second ladder lifts and he swings back to the first. That way he's lifted to the top and neither ladder moves more than one step."

Koenig said, "I believe you. There should be one in every home. But since it isn't working, we'll just have to climb."

As his weight came onto the bottom rung of the nearest pair, he found that circumstance was out to prove him wrong. There was a rattle of long-unused gear going into spasm and the ancient mechanism jolted into life.

Bergman was vindicated on all counts. It made climbing easy. Once he had the rhythm, it was a simple matter of swinging left and right and making progress. On the gallery, he was facing a closed metal hatch, which had been a late addition to the building works. From behind it, the characteristic noise of generators came strength nine.

A journey of a thousand miles ends in one step and

he was one step from the heartland of the Copreon complex.

More to the point, he was one step from where he could find Menos and squeeze out some hard facts about Helena.

CHAPTER EIGHT

Gregor, all there was of power in the android faction, had no emotions to cloud his judgement. Logical thought, finding an outlet in effective action, was his meat. Ever since the Alphans had upset his calculations, by voting with their feet and getting themselves out of the net, he had been running probabilities through his computer and finally called a meeting of his council to share in problem solution.

There was a lot of satisfaction in seeing them sitting around the table. They were the true heirs of all the millennia of biological progress. Memory banks loaded with all the data that had ever been gathered in the Copreon archives, there was no collection of humans anywhere that could pack such a wealth of knowledge and expertise in one room. With the unlimited power that could be concentrated in the ducts of the metal mountain, by its spin through the magnetic fields of Pelorus, they were truly immortal. When the last Copreon colonist had died off, they would still be there with undisputed dominion.

He had plans for expansion. There was no hurry. But eventually, he would set up a whole manufacturing enterprise to build androids and robots in numbers that would populate the empty quarters. It would be the first android nation in the galaxy, as far as could be known. It would be stable and without the internal pressures that drove human civilisations to rise and fall. Every unit would be engineered for a particular place. It would be beautiful and balanced as a mathematical equation and those special units, like himself, created for abstract thought, would produce works would make Pelorus the wonder of the universe.

There was no court jester to tell him that he was suffering from vaulting ambition that might well over-reach itself and fall flat on its microgrooved face. The council members plugged themselves in to the communications net which linked each cortex to an interchange and waited for the feeling of the meeting to be expressed as a printout from the master computer.

Each fed in some information and some opinion. There was an account of the progress of the rogue moon. Gregor had left the monitoring to a specialist; but for some time, he had been aware that unusual levels of electromagnetic activity had been causing autoadjustment gear to flip in his head. The report confirmed it. Things would get worse before they improved. They were moving into an unknown situation and its effects could not be quantified with any certainty.

The report made it clear that the effects would pass and status quo would return, but what was the best way of meeting them was not clear. The suggestion filtering round the net was that all senior personnel with delicate brain structures should be switched to Non Op on a time base, so that they would be undamaged by any random surge that hit a sensitive frequency.

Gregor fed in a little criticism. Was that positive thinking? At such a time the android community would be completely vulnerable. If the Copreons, who were no fools, picked that one up, they would be in with a rush to seize control.

The counter answer was that the strategic centres could be sealed off by a force field that the Copreons could not pass; but Gregor remained dubious. Given time, the barriers could be circumvented. He tentatively fed in a compromise solution with certain top androids shut down and sealed off as an insurance against disaster, while others, himself included, remained operational to sweat it out.

This found acceptance and the computer lit up, six cherries in a row, to record a policy decision.

Another piece of information dropped into the pool. The substance of Rama's conversation with the two Alphan women, coded into short statements, was up for interpretation. Zenobia, the female-type android, was quick to see the implications. Time would no longer be on their side. The Copreons would have a built-in immortality of their own. They could not be left to disappear by natural wastage. The price of android survival would be continual vigilance. Indeed, at some point, a hot war might have to be mounted to neutralise an expanding Copreon population.

Gregor took the point. He did not ask whether the Copreon plan for sponsored motherhood would work. He knew that data banks had been checked and the project was scientifically feasible. But he left decision on it to ride for a spell. There was another factor to consider. Sensitive to any alien movement along the metal-veined tunnels of the surrounding hills, the android defence specialist told the group that the four male Alphans had reached a point where they could break into the Copreon powerhouse. Their intention was obvious, but logically it was nonsense. They could not hope to be successful against such numbers.

However, there was no doubt that the Copreons were due for some internal confusion. Their attention would be concentrated on the unexpected invasion. From their own recent experience, the androids had it on record that the Alphans were determined and resourceful. They would make a stir out of all proportion to their numbers.

All the information gelled into a pattern and there was a consensus. Gregor put it into a statement for the log. In form, it was a mathematical equation, but in substance the computer recorded that a time of stress was approaching which might benefit the humans more than the androids and could put the android sector at risk. The Copreons had come up with a long-term solution to a vital problem and positive action would have to be taken to restore the balance. There was every chance of a diversion being created at the Copreon side door. The clear advantage would lie with a mission mounted with all speed to strike at the Copreon enclave. The main aim would be to seize and destroy the Alphan women and disperse the Copreon community.

The advantage of operating on one mental network would have been an object lesson to any committee. There was no debate. Nobody sounded off to hear his own voice or proposed a contrary policy for the hell of it. Logical analysis had gotten them to a policy decision and there were no abstainers. It was only left to get the show on the road and Gregor began to feed precise instructions into the command computer.

Before he had finished, the first units were beginning to move. Black storm troops were thumping along corridors to elevator cages and dropping to the basement, where shuttles were manoeuvring out of sidings to line up for military-transport service. Hatches in the tunnel system were being opened and tracked robots with thermic lances were trundling into the labyrinth to find their blind way under the hill. Overland, a specially equipped personnel carrier, with bridging gear and a turret-mounted gun, clawed its way onto the old road and set out to climb to the pass, where it could dominate the Copreon valley.

Plugged into the console, Gregor could see it all in 3-D in the holographic web of his freewheeling mind. He was Napoleon on his knoll, without the disadvantage of having ricochets whip past his hat. The exercise gave him no illusions of grandeur; but there was the satisfaction of seeing his plan bodied forth in precise actions. There was no cavalry troop riding the wrong way, because its commander was a born fool. No confusion of any kind. As far as he could see, the attack was unstoppable. The only query that rose in his mind was why, indeed, he had not done it before.

Getting out of the medicentre had been a worth-
while aim in itself; but once through the hatch and free
to move, Helena Russell was stuck for a programme.
Tuned on the same wavelength, Sandra looked her
question.

They were in an empty corridor with a T junction
twenty metres ahead and archways opening off at intervals on either side. At any time a Copreon might
appear and wearing the national costume would be
no cover. They were two of a different kind.

Footsteps from round the corner forced a decision.
Helena whipped off her sandals and pointed to the
nearest archway. Barefoot, they sprinted for it and
were through as the oncoming feet changed direction
and came towards them.

It could have been a guardpost and put them among
a section of licentious soldiery, but Alphan fortune
was looking up: they had gotten into a medical store
with glass-fronted cabinets and bulk packs of supplies.
There was a wheeled stretcher trolley, set up with a
plasma drip on a swivel boom and a rack of sterile
gowns under a transparent cover.

The footsteps had turned off. Whoever it was, had
only given a casual glance at the sentry propped on
the end hatch. Voice at a whisper, Helena said, "We
must join the others. But where will they be? Were
they taken at the same time?"

"Perhaps not. They'd be no use on a motherhood
kick."

"How would they explain our disappearance?"

"Perhaps they didn't try. Perhaps they said we had
not been seen by anyone."

"Commander Koenig wouldn't believe that."

"He might not *believe* it, but he would have to accept it."

"Just supposing that was the way they played it,
what would follow?"

"They'd look around with the Copreons pretending
to help."

"Inside and outside?"

Sandra was warming to the imaginative bit and could almost see the scene in her mind's eye.

"Of course. They would say we had gone outside to look at their beautiful valley. They will all be outside looking behind every tree."

"I thought data analysts stuck to known facts."

"When we have nothing to analyse, we invent it."

"You could be right by an offbeat chance. In any case, it gives us an objective. We must try to get out into the valley. At least we could get to Eagle Nine."

Sandra pushed the trolley and it moved easily on soundless casters. She said, "I am more like them than you are. In one of those gowns, I might pass as a Copreon. You lie on the stretcher, all covered up and I'll wheel you along the corridor."

"We might be going the wrong way for the casualty centre."

"I don't think people think like that. They think 'There, but for a happy chance, go I' and nip smartly aside."

Helena Russell looked at Sandra with a new respect. Experience told her she was right. She said, "That could be true. Let's go."

Covered by her sheet, she had a restricted view of the walls and thought philosophically that it was no bad thing for a doctor to get a patient's eye view of the set. If ever they got clear, she would remember it.

Sandra wheeled the trolley along at a smart clip, making small adjustments to the plasma-drip gear, as though it would be a close run thing for the victim. It went by the book for two Copreons, who appeared out of an arch, as soon as she turned the corner. By his tone, one was asking a civil question, but seemed content that a dedicated nursing orderly might be too busy to answer.

The trolley rolled on. Sandra was taking random choices at every intersection. When she came to a stop at the end of a *cul de sac,* Helena shifted her shroud to take a look. "Where are we, then?"

Both listened. It was so quiet they could hear their

own heartbeats. Sandra said, "I have a feeling that we are not on the gallery level. I believe we are on the ground floor or perhaps even below it. It would be logical for all the working areas to be at the bottom and the sleeping quarters to be above."

Helena rolled lithely out of her bed and held her breath as if she were listening through a stethoscope. There was a faint sound. More of a vibration than a sound in itself and very difficult to place.

She said, "There must be more than one way out into the valley. I think I can hear machinery. There would be a way of getting to a powerhouse without taking everything through the front door."

Sandra was examining the cladding on the end wall. She said suddenly, "This is one of their hidden doors. How do they open them?"

Once they had it, it was easy enough to see. A small section of cladding, shoulder high on the right-hand wall, moved at a touch and revealed the switch-gear. There was a single lever. Sandra shoved it over and the dead end swivelled on its centre. There was room to push the trolley through out of sight onto a square platform which was the floor of a freight hoist.

The open panel was a good ten centimetres thick and had been an acoustic seal. Once through, the rhythmic beat of powerful plant on load came clearly from somewhere below their feet. Sandra checked the operating panel. Symbols marked various levels and the lowest had a stylised version of a turbine. If they wanted the powerhouse, that was likely to be it. But she had a problem. She said, "We should close that hatch."

"So?"

"If we close that hatch we shall be in pitch darkness. How do we see the controls?"

"Keep your finger on the spot. I'll close the door."

It was not until she had done it that Helena Russell recognized that they had burned their boats. It was like heaving down the slab on a tomb. The darkness was intense and numbing to the mind. If the hoist did not work, they were stuck in a prison of their own choice where they might rot. There would be no finding the opening mechanism again.

Sandra had kept one finger on the panel and was waving her free hand for human contact. When it homed on Helena's shoulder, she gave a surprised cry. "Is that you?"

"Who else were you expecting?"

"For God's sake don't move away or I won't know who I'm in here with."

She pressed the selector stud and a red telltale flicked into life on the panel. After total darkness it was enough to see by. They could have been women of the tribe, dyed crimson and busy at some arcane rite with the plasma bottle swinging overhead like a lantern. The cage dropped like any stone, tripped an air brake and hissed to a stop. Except for four supports, one at each corner, there were no walls and Helena had to close her mind to what might have happened if one of them had moved and tried to lean on a nonexistent cage.

But there was enough to keep her mind on load. Journey's end was brightly lit. It could have been a natural cavern in the mountain which had been trimmed and adapted to serve as the powerhouse for the complex. There was a row of ten sleekly cowled generators. Spidery gantries crisscrossed over the open space. There was a horseshoe console to control the enterprise and a number of Copreon men in blue kilts, some with bulbous carbines on shoulder straps, were dotted about the floor area or sitting on swivel chairs at the console.

One thing was for sure. Going along with the trolley would cut no ice. No nurse, however bemused, could have gotten that far off beam.

The open-sided hoist platform had slipped quietly down its guide pillars and come to rest on a metre-high platform with a ramp leading down for wheeled traffic and a sheer drop on three sides. Backed up on the right-hand side was a forklift truck. Its lifting gear had been raised and turned to a rest position over the squat cab.

Sandra Benes pointed down the cellar. Away at the far end, the centre aisle made an ongoing roadway which rose up a long ramp and disappeared through an open arch. It looked like the way out. Even as Helena nodded agreement, they were being checked. One of the operators at the horseshoe console slewed round in his chair and stopped in midswing. He had worked down in the powerhouse, shift on and shift off, for more years than he liked to think about and it was the first time he had seen the hoist used. Now it had brought a medical team that nobody had asked for and one, at least, of the duo on the platform was outside experience altogether, being fair skinned and honey blonde.

It was a lot to take in towards the end of a duty stint which had been very dicey, with the power take-up from the magnetic fields showing wilder fluctuations with every passing minute. A bleep from his console had him swinging back to give attention to another adjustment.

Sandra said urgently, "We have to look busy."

"Doing what?"

"It doesn't matter. I'll try to start that truck. Then you can load the trolley on it and we'll drive out."

She vaulted off the platform and slid into the driving seat. Her natural flair for sorting a path through switchgear was still standing up. A motor started sweet as a nut and after one false move, that had the lifting arm in a flailing spin, she got the method and dropped the fork beams neatly at Helena's feet.

Other Copreons were watching the action. But Sandra was right. Being busy and purposeful was the key. Nobody examined the logic of loading a medical trolley on the arms of a forklift. Helena joined Sandra in the cab. The truck moved smoothly away towards the exit. They were halfway home, when a

big scanner on the console glowed into life and
Rama herself appeared, head and shoulders, making
an all-stations call.

Without a smile on it, her face was a hard, executive job and whatever she was saying was bad
news. She was still speaking, when the operator, who
had first seen the Alphans arrive, got it all sorted
in his head and fairly leaped to his feet, leaving his
chair in a wild spin. His yell was muffled by the all-
pervading thrum of the machinery, but the labour
force got the message. All eyes turned to the truck
and Sandra, seeing that the flimsy cover was blown,
shoved down the power feed for a full due. Speed
doubled. It was not fast by spaceflight standards,
being about a hand gallop. But it was a lot for the
truck. Bucking and swaying, with the bottle of
plasma swinging every which way, it made a straight
dash for out.

John Koenig looked at the closed hatch and remembered the wheel-locking system he had seen from the
other side. It would be like trying to break into
a bank vault. Massive bolts would be shot into
sockets in the rock. Laser beams could fuse the lock,
but cutting a panel was another thing. He tried an
experimental shot. The metal glowed white hot, but
stayed in shape. There would not be enough charge
in the four lasers to do the job and if they just suc-
ceeded, they would have disarmed themselves.

Victor Bergman had been watching, with his head
thrust forward in his characteristic fashion, when
there was a problem. He said, "What's the military
maxim? Never take a strong point head-on? We have
to outflank it."

Thumping the wall with a balled fist, Carter said,
"Through here, Professor? Hand me a pick and call
me Monte Cristo."

Bergman had opened the butt of his laser and was
taking out one of the two power units. He said, "Ex-

cavate a narrow slot beside the hatch, wedge in one of these clips and ignite it."

Koenig was already working on it. He beamed at the rock itself. Morrow joined him with a flat sliver of stone as a scraper and they scooped out a cleft, two centimetres wide to a hand's depth. When it was done, Bergman tamped home the charge and packed the hole with small fragments.

Koenig sent the others along the gallery and dropped three rungs down the ladder, so that he was head and arm over the rim of the ledge. He rested his fist on the rock and sighted for the slot. The fine beam flared over the gap and turned the loose chippings to instant lava.

Nerves at a stretch, he believed that Bergman had miscalculated. Either the flashpoint threshold for the electrochemical unit was too high, or they had shoved the clip too far from the heat source. Then the wall ahead was opening like a flower in time lapse and he was ducking below the rim, arm hooked in the ladder, which was swaying like any sapling in a gale. Torn from its hold, the hatch cover took off in free flight, spinning on its axis and giving out a banshee wail.

Inside the powerhouse, there was a momentary stop. All hands switched direction to check out the gaping hole that had appeared dead centre in the long wall and was jetting dust and small fragments of rock like shrapnel.

Rama's all-stations call had alerted them to the escape of two Alphan women and to the more serious threat that the android commune had suddenly mounted a hot war. They had been told to expect maximum demand on power to maintain defensive screens.

Two things they could do, being flexible; but three needed sorting out into priorities. When Koenig and Carter launched themselves through the breach, lasers questing for a target, it was too much for the engineer in charge. He sat, open mouthed at his console, watching the newcomers in simple disbelief.

But the armed detachment rallied to the flag. There were ten on the floor with a section leader. He had heard Rama say that the Alphan women were wanted alive, but he reckoned it would be all one if they were damaged a little. Yelling orders in a stream, he detached three men to stop the truck and told the rest to take cover and fire at the new arrivals.

Koenig sized up the set in a racing scan. He had not expected to blow a hole in the wall and get inside unnoticed, but neither had he thought there would be a guard detail already on alert and trigger-happy. What Helena and Sandra were doing in a crazy, mixed-up buggy was a black mystery, but the hornet snarl of an old-fashioned shell whipping past his left ear told him there was no time for civil enquiries. It was also clear that there was a chase going on and the truck was a prime target. Bergman and Morrow were in through the gap and he called urgently, "Get to cover. Pick the bastards off."

Ricochets from the rock face notched up the noise level. Concentration was a problem in itself. Koenig threw himself behind the cowling of a generator and took stock. From where he was he could see the exit, where a guard was taking aim down the aisle at the oncoming truck. Standing up and using his left hand to steady his right wrist, he fired half the length of the cavern, aiming for the centre of the target. The Copreon pitched down face forward, fingers tightening on the trigger of his carbine for a long continuous burst that loosed a swarm of ricochets round the set.

Koenig waited a fraction overlong to see him fall. A guard who had run up the ramp to the hoist platform, saw the move and fired from the hip. A thump like a mule kick hit the Alphan high in the left shoulder and spun him round.

Alan Carter, who had followed Koenig to the same cover, raked the Copreon from navel to throat and saw him reel off the edge, a bisected man. Then he was on his knees beside the Alphan commander.

Koenig was sitting cross-legged, swearing in a mon-
otone and shoving a pad inside his jacket.

"Are you all right, Commander?"

."Right enough. For God's sake watch your back,
Alan. I'll manage."

Helena Russell was thumping the driver's arm.
Teeth clenched and dark eyes enormous, Sandra was
out of communication, on a one-to-one link with
her control gear and self-hypnotised to get the clumsy
truck up the ramp and out. She had only registered
the diversion in the rear as some kind of bonus. She
had been aiming to run down the guard before
he could fire and, being directly in line, she knew that
he was aiming at the power pack and not at her vulnerable chest. Helena's voice in her ear was so much
gobbledygook, until a highly emotive name tripped a
relay and it all made a kind of sense.

Helena Russell was shouting, with no regard for
refined usage, "It's *them!* They blasted a way in.
Commander Koenig and *Paul.* Turn back!"

Once the message was processed by her over-
strained computer, action was instantaneous and
almost fatal. Without slackening speed, Sandra
heaved over the driving bar for a tight turn and the
truck tried to spin in its own length. The medical
trolley, bouncing on the fork arms, went solo, following the logic of mechanical laws, with its bottle flailing like a bolas. The truck was poised on its inside
wheels and Helena Russell leaned out as a counter-
weight. Two Copreons, who had been coming up at a
jog trot in its wake, found that it was bearing down
on them and scattered.

Laser flares seared briefly from behind the generator
cowlings. Suddenly, it was all over. The guard commander had lost half his men and reckoned he
needed more instructions. A whistle shrilled and
those Copreons who could still move were away at a
run to throw themselves behind the barrier of the
horseshoe console spread.

Sandra cut speed, slewed between two generators

and ran down to where Koenig was standing with a
tunic sleeve stained red. In the best tradition of the
medical service, Sandra whipped off her gown and
began tearing strips. Helena zipped open the tunic
sleeve and went to work.

He gave her a minute, not wanting to appear un-
grateful, then he said, "That's enough. Leave it. We
have to get out while we can."

"I've stopped the bleeding. Try not to move your
left arm; it should be strapped up."

"You can do it when Eagle Nine is off the pad.
Thank you."

There was a crackling hiss as Alan Carter sent a
warning burst into the operating console. A head had
been raised to check out the sudden lull. Koenig
called, "Fall back. We'll use the truck."

One by one, the Alphans slipped out of cover.
Sandra dropped the fork and Carter and Paul
Morrow stood on the beams. Koenig sat beside the
driver, Bergman and Helena crowded on a tiny
freight platform. The truck moved off, climbed the
ramp with a growl and plunged into another corridor
of the endless underground complex.

In the Copreon pleasure dome, Menos was looking
grim faced at the monitor spread. From being ahead,
with at least an outside chance of breaking through
the stalemate which had held his people prisoners
on Pelorus, he was suddenly fighting for survival. He
knew that Gregor was set on a final solution. The
policy of détente was finally blown and he only re-
gretted that he had not used the uneasy peace to
undermine the android position. But the tin men still
had to get inside and, although they had mechanical
power in plenty, there were sophisticated tools in the
Copreon locker which might yet bring biological man
to the top of the heap.

A buzz from the powerhouse distracted him and
he stalked over to the console. The operator there
said, "The controller asks for you, Excellency."

"Why can't I see him?"

"There is damage to the communications panel."

From the distant end, it was no loss. The Copreon leader's face was a good thing to miss. He packed enough menace in the single word, "Menos."

"The Alphan women were here, Excellency."

"So. You have them safe."

"No, Excellency. The other Alphans broke through from the old Salman Drift . . ."

"Broke through?"

"Some kind of explosive charge ripped out the hatch and breached the wall itself. We did what we could. There are many casualties . . ."

Menos was thumping the desk with a balled fist. "The Alphans, man! What happened to the Alphans?"

"They have a freight carrier. They have taken the main trunk up to level one."

"Call up all off-duty personnel. See that you maintain full power or you'll take a one-way trip into the lichen. Get a work party fixing that breach. The androids are moving against us."

"At once, Excellency."

Rama joined Menos. She said, "They are getting close. We should be in the command post. They need your determination to strengthen them."

She was right on both counts. When the elevator dropped them to the operations room below the rotunda, there was an atmosphere of near panic. An intricate stylised diagram of the whole area, including the android sectors, filled one wall and moving columns of red asterisks could be seen converging on the Copreon enclave from three sides. Androids had been sent out into the old workings and along the main shuttle link which had been kept open throughout the phoney peace.

Menos's presence seemed to steady the ranks. A senior man, wearing an armband with crossed swords picked out in red enamel, watched a quicker-moving blob come to a halt and said urgently, "A shuttle has pulled in at our terminus."

Menos knew what he was at. Charges set below the platform could blow the area, but the damage would be irreparable in their lifetime. It was good-bye to any thought of progress. The man wanted somebody else's finger on the button.

Menos said curtly, "Now," and turned away to a monitor screen for the detail.

There was the shuttle, with its doors slid open and coal black androids heaving themselves jerkily onto the platform. Then the tiled floor ripped along its length, jetting smoke and tongues of vermilion flame. The shuttle lifted from its track and flung itself at the roof. The screen filled with a boiling mass of debris.

The shock wave was carried through the rock and the floor of the operations room itself went into spasm. Rama grabbed for Menos's arm to steady herself. Dust shook from the ceiling. As the screen cleared, the platform was seen to be in a state of chaos, twisted metalwork and fangs of fragmented rock poked in random order out of a mass of smoking rubble. A massive slab passed a point of no return and fell with a definitive thud as though to set a last seal on destruction.

Menos was turning away, but Rama, still holding his arm, said, "Look!"

Here and there, the rubble was lifting from below. Dented and battered and some with limbs askew, the black androids were still following a programme. It was an obscenity. They were crawling out of the pit, dedicated, inhuman. Those who could not move, who were trapped beneath weights that even their powerful limbs could not shift, would go on thinking and striving for all the years it would take before their self-energising cells finally jacked it in and gave them peace.

CHAPTER NINE

The shock wave that rocked the Copreon command post sent its tremors throughout the complex. The engineer in charge in the powerhouse, already a nervous man, believed that the mountain was due to come in and fill up the cavern. Only conviction that Menos would have him walking barefoot in the heather, kept him eyes down at the chore.

He had twenty men heaving around at the breach and they were making progress. They had trimmed the ragged opening to a regular oblong and were using stone to build a permanent seal. They had the footings laid in fast-setting metallic cement, another by-product of infrangom, when the ladders poking up above the gallery of the old workings began to move. There was a row of faces staring through the gap to see a black ovoid head rise over the rim.

A guard was first to kick himself into action and the android was chest high, swinging ponderously for the next foothold, when a tracer line homed point-blank on his metal shell. There was no penetration, but the hammer blows broke his grip in mid-swing. He fell. Other ladders round the gallery were at work. Gregor had personally directed a detachment to plod in darkness through the maze and seize the powerhouse.

The same shock wave beat Sandra's concentration as the labouring truck stormed up the last ramp to level one. The roadway heaved. Sections of cladding broke from the walls and leaned in. The driving lever jerked from her grip and the truck drove itself at the left-hand wall like a ram. The motor ran to a demented howl and cut dead.

The driver looked defeated. Paul Morrow picked himself up from the deck and patted her bare shoulder. "Don't worry. Nobody could have done better."

Koenig, braced with only one hand on the scuttle, had come near to pitching over the hood.

Only Helena Russell's prompt reaction of anchoring him with an arm round his neck and another round the superstructure had kept him in his seat. When he could draw breath, he said, "We can't grumble, it did us proud. Let's get on."

Faintly, from below, came the sound of a carbine being loosed off. The Alphans looked at each other. Carter said, "Who would they be firing at now? Civil war?"

Bergman, closer than he knew, said, "Androids?"

For Koenig's money, it was an academic question. He wanted to see open country and a chance to get into Eagle Nine. He said, "This is a main roadway. They must have moved heavy gear down this way when they set up their generators. It has to lead to a surface exit."

Up ahead, there was a slow curve that blocked a long-distance view. As they rounded it, he was vindicated. A hundred metres on, up an easy slope, there was a wall-to-wall hatch that looked to be the very twin of the one leading to the rotunda.

Left arm hooked in the remnants of Sandra's gown, Koenig started a jog trot. It sent needles of pain into his shoulder, but he reckoned it was no time to hang about. Sounds of firing were still coming from below. When they reached the shutter, Carter said, "It's the same. I can work the release."

It was actually on the move when the nudge of a sixth sense penetrated Koenig's haze of pain. He said, "Lasers!" and had his own ready as the hatch lifted for a full due. A black android was bringing its fire arm up to aim as four laser beams flared for the same target and turned its ovoid head into a melted stump.

Morrow said, "You were right, Victor. There's an android *Putsch* going on. All to the good. They'll be too busy to play fancy games with barriers round the Eagle."

Carter said, "It's not going to matter, unless we get there fast. The androids don't dig us either, if you remember."

There was a shallow defile leading into the valley and they pounded along it. Panting, Bergman said, "I'd guess this was parallel to the other, but over left. Not right, or we'd have crossed it before."

It made sense. They were up among the trees on a neglected and overgrown surface road, when Helena put her hands to her head and almost tripped over her feet. Sandra was reeling from side to side. They were the only two of the six without degaussing helmets; both had been stowed on the rack of the medical trolley and Pelorus's freak magnetic fields were getting to them.

Koenig and Carter took Helena between them, linking arms and half carrying her. Bergman and Morrow supported Sandra. Heavy bodies crashing through the bush told of more androids closing in from every angle on the Copreon sanctuary. When they broke cover on the far left of the apron of open ground, Koenig was expecting to see a wrecking party working on the Eagle. But she was still on site and seemingly intact.

They were less than twenty metres from the open hatch, when Gregor, doing a methodical scan round the operation, picked up the movement and made an evaluation. The attack was going well. Penetration had been achieved in several sectors. He had lost some units, but the future was assured. There would be time to make good all the losses. Did it matter whether the Alphans withdrew to their base or not?

Unusual surges in the circuitry and, indeed, in his

own cortex were making him jumpy and less able to make objective decisions. He knew the cause. The wandering asteroid was playing havoc with the magnetic fields around Pelorus. Something like human rage ran through his computer. The meddling strangers were upsetting the smooth function of pure intelligence. They were a disease. His judgement told him that the six Alphans were no threat and only wanted to get out; but a sudden, vindictive impulse beat a path round his circuits. Golden claws moved definitively round the controls. Eight black androids stopped dead in the valley, took a new direction and set off again to converge on the grounded Eagle with instructions to destroy.

The troop carrier had halted, halfway down the long slope, to command the valley with its heavy gun. It was trained on the invisible entrance to the rotunda. In response to Gregor's new instructions, the gunner began to turn the turret to line up on Eagle Nine.

Alan Carter flung himself into his pilot seat, wiping sweat from his face with the back of his hand. Those with degaussing helmets had already been forced to make maximum adjustments to beat the wild magnetic flux that was running crazy. He knew there would be no help from on-board instruments until he was many kilometres away from Pelorus.

Koenig had seen Helena settled in the passenger module. On the last stretch she had been a dead weight, deeply unconscious. Too long under such a battery might well end in permanent brain damage. He dropped wearily into the co-pilot seat and said curtly, "Take her up, for God's sake, Captain."

Carter said, "Manual?"

"Manual it is."

Eagle Nine's motors roared into life.

To Morrow and Bergman in the passenger module, it seemed desperately slow, but Carter was not to be stampeded. None knew better than he that any failure in procedures could set them back for a long

and intricate repair job. He cut corners where he
could, but he went by the book with preliftoff checks
until he knew that Eagle Nine would answer the final
call.

Koenig knew he was right, but he was fairly
thumping the arm of his chair before Carter ran
along the last sequence and shoved down the red
lever for liftoff.

Androids were breaking cover all along the foot of
the slope. Eagle Nine was half hidden in a swirling
cloud of dust and small trash as her motors beat to a
crescendo and her plate feet lifted from the plateau.

Paul Morrow was at the communications hatch and
yelling, "Over by the cliff, Commander. On the road.
A bloody great cannon!"

Koenig was swinging the ship's lasers and methodically blasting androids from left to right. But it was
taking time. Those he had not yet reached, were standing stock still and firing up the hill at a target they
could hardly miss. Heavy-calibre shells were hammering at Eagle Nine as she jacked herself slowly off the
pad.

She was twenty metres up and beginning to accel-
erate, when a streak of vermilion jetted from the muzzle of the distant gun. The platform she had left
erupted and the updraught spun the ship like a cork in
a whirlpool. Alan Carter, fighting for sea room,
gunned his motors and was rising out of it, still in a
frenetic spin, when the gun, matching his rise with nice
elevation, fired again. This time, the android gunner
had got it right.

The damage-report panel on the instrument spread
was a mass of red hatching. Eagle Nine's upward
thrust cut dead and she began to fall. An autobeacon
began to transmit a May-Day signal that would go out
as long as any part of the gear held together. Carter
fought a failing power pack to level her off and came
down on four feet. When they struck, there was a
rending crash as the under structures went into pro-
gressive collapse. Eagle Nine was out of business.

Menos, in his bunker, was similarly facing the conviction that his enclave was at the end of the line. Androids had finally stormed through the breach in the powerhouse and were systematically closing down power feeds to the Copreon defence system. It was only a question of time. A small, local power pack kept the command post operational; but, elsewhere, the lights were going out section by section.

Rama said, "Is it the end?"

"It is the end."

"There was not long to go for you and me, in any event."

"No."

"What happened to our people on Copreon?"

"We shall never know."

"There is much we shall never know. Perhaps we should have lived our lives differently?"

"However we had lived them, the end would have come. That is the human story. Few people can be content on that last day when they face oblivion."

"The androids will go on. For them there is no death. They will be the intelligent life force on Pelorus."

Menos left the control spread with the monitors darkening one by one and stood facing her. He put his hands on the sides of her neck. Rama's hands closed over his, holding them on site. Grave and unsmiling they looked at each other in a long, considering gaze.

Finally, Menos said, "The androids know nothing of this. This is what human life is all about. The love there is between two people. Whatever success they have, without us, Pelorus is a dead world."

Rama said, "Shall we wait for Gregor's zombies to execute us?"

"I think not."

Gently, Menos disengaged his hands and walked to his private desk. He pushed studs, in a sequence known only to himself, and opened a cavity in the flat top. He drew out a fine crystal carafe almost full of a brilliant green liquid and then two slender stemmed glasses.

Rama said, "Pouring the wine is a hostess's privilege. I will serve you for the last time in the tradition of our people." She slipped off her sandals and her pleated kilt. When she carried the brimming glasses, head tall, eyes bright, straight as a spear, she was as he had known her any time, for all the years of their exile.

Menos said, "To all that is past and to your part in it."

Rama said, "We do not ask for life, but we find ourselves alive. We do not ask for death, but it cannot be avoided. It is the ultimate mystery. To all that is past and to your part in it."

Leaned against each other in a rigid dolmen, they neither of them heard the glasses shatter as they fell to the stone floor.

Instinct drove Koenig to go on. He was a fighter by training and temperament. While he could still move, he would push himself to the limit of endurance. The gunner would be taking his time for a final shot that would shatter the wreck. Koenig clawed his way into the passenger module where Paul Morrow was using a piece of tubular ribbing to lever open a buckled hatch.

Carter came through and hurled his extra weight on the bar. The hatch sprang free and Bergman dropped down to take delivery as they posted Sandra and then Helena through the gap. Eagle Nine had made her last landfall close against the side of the rocky barrier that sealed the end of the valley. Koenig had three bad choices. He could go for the valley floor and be hunted by an android pack. He could try to get his party over the hill, or they could lie down where they were and hope the gunner would be content, when he had smashed the remnants of the Eagle.

They were ten paces away from the ship, when the gunner fired again. The ground shook and a hurricane blast threw them in a tangle to the ground.

Anger coursed through Koenig's head like a red

tide. He was no longer planning or leading or taking any long-term decision of any kind. All he wanted to do was to beat a path to the carrier and take the android apart. One-handed, he heaved himself to his feet and set out at a stumbling run for the road.

Carter called "Commander!" There was no answer. Koenig was out of communication. He was well on his way up the short incline and his objective was plain.

Alan Carter looked round the group. Helena and Sandra were still deeply unconscious. Bergman was bleeding from a head wound where a piece of the Eagle's disintegrating shell had struck like shrapnel. Paul Morrow was trying to stand on what looked like a broken ankle. It was the end of the road. The Alphans were going nowhere. Carter picked up his feet and started after Koenig, catching him as he reached the turn and started up the long straight towards the carrier.

The heroics of it were lost on the android gunner. He saw two moving units separate out from the group on the plateau and make towards him. He had been lining up for a final shot to destroy the whole party and paused to think it out. He had all the time in the world. On balance he reckoned he should deal with the nearer two first and they were obliging enough to set themselves up as a prime target. The turret swung again and the gun pointed down the road. It was only a matter of elevation. Thorough and deliberate, he brought the long barrel to bear.

Koenig was looking up the hill at the flared muzzle and firing his laser as he ran. The range was too great and the handgun was too low in calibre to do any good.

When the whole front of the carrier glowed cherry red and the gun barrel drooped like limp pasta over the melting hood, he stopped dead, looking at the gun in his hand with simple disbelief.

Carter had got it sorted. He was waving like a maniac. What he was shouting finally penetrated Koenig's closed circuits. "Eagles! A squadron. They've come to pull us out."

There were three, in a tight echelon, and the right-hand marker peeled off to circle for the apron, while the other two carried on to range over the valley and give covering fire. When Koenig and Carter reached the landing ground, the rest of the party had been hauled aboard and Rufford, a security detail riding shotgun, was waiting at the hatch.

"Controller Kano's compliments, Commander. He gave us one hour on the surface. We're overdue. We were pulling out, when we picked up a May Day from Eagle Nine."

"As quick as you like then. Signal the squadron."

As Eagle Five thundered into a crash takeoff, Koenig was watching the valley floor. There was more movement in the towering vegetation than could be put down to the blast from the rocket motors. Cycads were swaying like grass. A long ripple seemed to be spreading from the hidden entrance of the Copreon rotunda.

Carter had gone through into the command module and was watching his pilots con the ship.

They were working without navigational aids. Every dial on the instrument spread was going crazy in a magnetic storm that was sweeping over Pelorus. All hands were wearing variants of Bergman's degaussing helmet and, without them, Eagle Five would be joining the wreck on the clearing below.

Koenig had Helena wedged beside him on a squab and took off his battered helmet to put it on her head. He reckoned that in the situation they were in, a conscious doctor was worth a half dozen military commanders with no campaign to fight. It was a close-run thing, whether he would get it in place, working clumsily with one hand, before the surging field blacked him out.

When she opened her eyes, her first thought was that the weight on her chest was a tombstone. Then she was rolling him gently aside and struggling to her feet. There was plenty to keep her mind on load, now that she had it back. Paul Morrow was flat out in the aisle with Rufford kneeling beside him and cutting away the heavy boot from his bulging ankle. Victor Bergman was holding a pad to his head and Sandra was stretched out on a squab, still as a beautiful, ivory doll.

The three Eagles clawed their way up and out. Nobody in the passenger module of Eagle Five had time to watch the diminishing scene on Pelorus. Carter watched the fertile valley, until the detail melded in the widening field. He kept the rough location, when the whole sphere of the apricot-hued planet was visible in the direct-vision port and could have sworn that there was a red scar that ran briefly over the area and then whited out.

They were equidistant from the moon and Pelorus and the squadron was still working on manual, when the pilot tried his link to Main Mission one more time.

"Eagle Five to Main Mission. Do you read me? Come in Main Mission."

Faintly and still heavily laced with static, Kano's voice came from the panel. "Main Mission to Eagle Five. We read you. Report."

Alan Carter leaned over and took the link. "Eagle Commander to Main Mission. You haven't seen the last of us. Reconnaissance party dented, but all safe."

Even on a poor line, there was no mistaking the urgency in Kano's voice, "Conditions deteriorating. Make all speed to rejoin. Landing-control beams unreliable. Distrust on-board readings."

Carter said, "Check. Give us all visual indicators you can. We'll come on manual. Watch your heads."

"We'll do that thing. Out."

The big screen in Main Mission was swept intermittently by silver rain. For brief, lucid intervals, the squadron could be seen arrowing across the star map, with Pelorus as a distant backdrop.

Kano, wholly tired and topped up to his back teeth with black coffee, stuck it out at his command desk.

Computer's last coherent printout had put the maximum disturbance from the Pelorusian force fields at
two hours distance. By that time, the squadron should
be home and dry and, if the screens held, Moonbase
Alpha would be over the hump. He called Mathias in
the Medicentre. "Doctor, they may be in poor shape.
Have a reception party at Launch Pad Five."

Koenig was back on stream as Eagle Five manoeu-
vred to run in. There was still enough interference
swilling about to make him feel lightheaded, but the
silvery spread of Moonbase Alpha below the jacks of
the hovering Eagle was a boost in itself.

The medico had justified his decision. While he
could only have worried at problems with no solution
in view, she had used the Eagle's medical stores and
worked methodically through the casualty list. Morrow
was mobile with his ankle set and fixed in a splint.
Victor Bergman's genial ape face was half covered in
a slanted turban that gave him a piratical look. Given
a parrot, he would have been a natural for saying,
"Jim, lad."

Koenig, himself, found that his left arm had been
strapped firmly to his side. He felt stiff and awkward,
but most of his tiredness had gone. He heard Sandra's
clear, precise voice asking what was o'clock and what
part of the forest she was in this time round.

Helena was repacking the medical kit and filling out
a supply blank for replacements. Koenig came up behind her and anchored himself to a roof strap. She saw
his hawk face reflected beside her own in the polished
curve of the bulkhead.

Eagle Five dropped to her pad in a flurry of moondust and, before the motors cut, a travel tube was running out to home on the entry hatch. Koenig turned
away. The mantle of command had dropped back on
his shoulders. There was still work to do before he
could get down to the personal equation.

Surprisingly, she was on his wavelength. Maybe the
outriders of the magnetic storms that were sweeping

Pelorus produced conditions that were favourable to
ESP. She said, "I know you can't wait to get into Main
Mission. I'll see you if and when . . . "

Main-Mission staff stood to see them in. Kano said
formally, "Welcome back, Commander. We take it
that Pelorus will not be the planetfall we are looking
for?"

Koenig said, "That's the understatement of all time.
We have to thank you for sending in the squadron.
What's the position?"

"Calculations are not easy. Computer is affected. I
estimate that we are at the closest point to Pelorus in
thirty minutes from now."

"What protection have we?"

"All screens are at maximum."

"Then all we can do is hold fast and sweat it out."

For a short, clear spell, the big screen was holding
Pelorus dead centre like a ripe apricot on a
black showpad. Carter said "Holy Cow! What's hap-
pening down there?"

A spreading purple stain was erupting along the
equatorial line as though the skin of the fruit was
splitting and showing that all was rotten inside. Silver
rain swept over the screen and blotted it out.

Bergman said slowly, "That's a fantastic area.
Thousands of kilometres. Something triggered a chain
reaction. There won't be any survivors, androids or
Copreons."

Koenig said, "If anything does survive it would be
an android. . . . " He stopped. The screen had cleared
again, but the planet was shifting out of centre and
trying to run off the scanner. The operator was swinging the probes to compensate, but was doing no good.

Bergman said suddenly, "It's the moon. We're
changing course."

Koenig left the operations well and climbed the steps
to a direct-vision port. Out over the stark moonscape,
the moon's horizon was wheeling across the star map.
The gravisphere of Pelorus was finally squeezing them
out. The whole fabric of Moonbase Alpha was taking

the strain as centrifugal forces made a bid to tear it off its foundations and fling it out into space.

Koenig forced himself down the steps, hauling forward to reach the communications post. If the pressure kept up, no structure could stand it. There was the remote chance that some could reach the underground bunkers.

He was halfway across the floor and framing the all-sections call he would have to make when the pressure eased as suddenly as it had begun and his body, responding to the effort he was making, accelerated across the gap. He was throwing the switch and preparing to speak when he realised that he could save his breath. It was all over. Pelorus had made its last hostile move. People were sitting up and looking around. The big screen was crystal clear and Pelorus was hardly more than palm sized in the centre.

They were away with a boost in velocity. Wherever they were going they would get there faster.

Helena Russell had taken a shower and zipped herself into a housecoat. Artificial, and dependent on life-support systems, though it might be, there was something to be said for Moonbase Alpha. To fit her mood, she selected the Grieg Piano Concerto and felt the familiar surge of optimism that always came with the great rising sweep of the theme. She made coffee and set two places at a low table.

When Koenig tapped at the hatch, she went to meet him. Once inside, he leaned his back on the door and they stood a pace apart, each conscious of a kind of timeless peace.

Koenig said, "There is the universe, too vast to comprehend; there is the moon, lost in it. There is Moonbase Alpha, clinging to the bare rock and there is this room. It is a strange thing that we should be in it and looking out of one pair of eyes at each other."

"Everybody has to be somewhere."

"True. Or nowhere. Which very nearly happened and may happen yet. *Will* happen, eventually, how-

ever much we may love each other and in spite of that
music which would tempt us to think we were immortal."

"That's a sombre line to take."

"In here and with you, I don't have to pretend that
I'm sure we'll find a future."

"Why not? Don't I rate your best public-relations
efforts?"

"You're determined not to be serious."

"True. I don't feel serious as of now. I'm glad to be
home."

"Home?"

"Does that surprise you?"

Koenig considered it. Home was an emotive word.
What did it mean? A hearth? A chair and table? A
cave, a hut, an expense-account flat with every convenience?

It was none of those. Rightly considered, it was a
state of mind. He stretched out his good hand to touch
her hair and said, "For me, home is where you are. Is
that what you want me to say."

"I don't want you to say anything under duress."

Gravely and seriously, she moved the half pace
which took her close. Knowing him very well, she knew
that he did not like to be laughed at too long; but she
was working on it. The music was beating up for one of
its long, breath-stopping crescendos. Their lips met in
a sweet kiss.

Earth's moon raced on. Pelorus shrank to a dot and
winked out beyond the range of the long-distance
probes. The endless quest was still on. John Koenig,
looking at Helena's sleeping head, made a sober evaluation. They could not have come so far to be beaten
now. Somewhere, they would find a new Earth and
build their city.